The Emotional Embodiment of Stars

A Collection of Short Stories

Lune Spark Books, Morrisville, NC

All the characters, names, places, and incidents appearing in this work are the product of the authors' imagination. Any resemblance to real persons, living or dead, events, or locales is entirely coincidental.

Publisher: Lune Spark LLC

PO Box 1443, Morrisville, NC, 27560, United States

www.lunespark.com

Young Writers' Resources: www.lunespark.com/youngwriters

E-mail: books@lunespark.com

Phone: +1 (919) 809-4235

Ordering Information: Quantity sales. Special discounts are available on quantity purchases by corporations, associations, and others. For details, contact the publisher at the address above.

Or visit www.lunespark.com.

Hardback ISBN 13: 978-1-947960-21-3

Paperback ISBN 13: 978-1-947960-20-6

eBook ISBN 13: 978-1-947960-22-0

Library of Congress Control Number: 2018952128

Lune Spark Books, Morrisville, NC

Cover art by Maya Lewins

1. Short Stories 2. Anthology 3. Creative writing 4. Young writers

First edition

To the young writers whose storytelling talent is yet to be discovered. May the world find you soon!

"Most of the basic material a writer works with is acquired before the age of fifteen." - Willa Cather

Contents

Introduction

I can't be more proud of the talented young writers of the stories in this book. This year's *Lune Spark Short Story Contest* saw a long list of splendid stories. While the judges couldn't have been happier enjoying each one of those stories, it made their job harder in distinguishing one good story from another. We can all certainly agree that's a great problem to have, for it speaks volumes of the talent our next generation of writers is going to have.

Our esteemed judges picked the top twenty-five stories to publish in each of the two contest categories, *10–12 Years* and *13–15 Years*, so that these fantastic stories from promising young writers can reach even more readers and they get the recognition they deserve.

Starting this year, we are also ensuring we group the stories by age for our target readers. *The Emotional Embodiment of Stars* contains stories appropriate for young adults—readers above the age of thirteen. The other stories are simultaneously published in a separate anthology called *Speaking Up for Each Other,* which is appropriate for tweens and middle grade readers.

Wonderfully wide-ranging, original, and enjoyable, this outstanding collection features twenty-seven short stories like *Mortimer*, in which an unwanted guest secretly follows a family through their heartbreaking sorrows and *Crossroads*, in which a budding writer is finally preparing to meet the man she happens to exchange greetings with every morning on the way to her office.

My special gratitude goes to the following people without whose help it wouldn't have been possible to run the contest and publish this book.

- The participants of the 2018 Lune Spark Short Story Contest and their parents for all the enthusiasm and support.
- The judges of the 2018 contest: Alexandra Hubbell, Simon Brading, Kenneth Preston, SF Benson, Mbangohol Ikeseh, and James Hockley.

Last but not the least, a constant encouragement from their readers is the best thing that can happen to these young writers in their journey to becoming seasoned writers. So if you like their work, please allow your appreciation to reach them in the form of a review on the book websites or on your blogs. Rest assured that these talented young writers will very eagerly be reading every single review, looking for encouragement and constructive criticism.

Let me disappear now so that I do not come in between you and these wonderful stories. Happy reading!

—Pawan Mishra, Morrisville, North Carolina
August 2018

Crossroads

Laura Cao

That day, he wrapped a scarf around her neck. A bright red scarf.

My name is Hannah. I'm a writer. Well, almost. My first novel…it's still incomplete. Meanwhile I work at a publishing house as a marketing clerk in order to support my ambitions of becoming an author and, frankly, to survive. It's a physically and mentally draining job. Ten-hour shifts of answering phone calls, typing out long documents, and running coffee errands for higher-ups, all while being surrounded by people who once had the same hopes and dreams I have but ended up working jobs like *this* for meager pay. The pay is really nothing to brag about—it's enough to get the rent paid, and I'm happy with that. I'm a country girl so moving to such a big city was a daunting experience. I don't have any friends or family here. It gets lonely, I admit.

I usually leave my apartment at seven o'clock in the morning. I catch the seven fifteen bus, which drops me off outside a park with a vast weeping willow, its branches flowing over the front gates. Then I walk to the train station. Every day, on my way to the station, I'll pass through a crossroads. The pedestrian lights turn green at exactly seven thirty. It's there where I met him.

I see him every day at the crossing. He's tall and has a handsome face. He has a light brown satchel casually strung over his shoulder. On cold days, hung loosely around his neck is a red scarf.

After we both realized how often we'd pass each other, simply walking on turned into a small nod of acknowledgment. A nod turned into a shy smile. A smile turned into a "hi." The "hi" then became a "good morning." Small steps, small steps.

It's a busy crossroads. Thousands of people must walk past every day. Strange, that the two of us would always manage to walk beside each other. Strange that he chose to notice me out of all those people, me who had never stood out in any way, who wasn't that pretty or attractive.

Seeing this person became a highlight of my life. It started to become something I looked forward to every morning. I would purposely leave my home a few minutes early so that I wouldn't miss seeing him at seven thirty. Because he would always be there with a warm smile. I didn't know who he was, where he was from, where he was going. But when he smiled at me, all my worries about not finishing my novel, paying rent, my scattered thoughts and anxieties seemed to be less of a problem. He was something stable in my simple but chaotic life.

~~~

Yesterday morning was bitterly cold and dismal. Icy wind slapped across my face as I walked hurriedly on my way to the station. I had woken up late and, in my rush, forgotten my coat. As usual, he and I passed side by side, greeted each other, and carried on.

"Wait!"

I spun around, surprised. He was walking back toward me! My heart pounded erratically in my chest like it was trying to escape, so loudly I was sure he would be able to hear it. He stopped in front of me, took off his red scarf, and draped it carefully around my neck.

"The weather's bad today. You might catch a cold." He smiled and then walked away.

I was so speechless I forgot to say thank you. Was this real? It was like one of the princes from a childhood fairy tale popped out into reality.

I stood there in a daze for a while, when suddenly I heard my name being called. Turning around, I saw one of my
~~~

coworkers, Carrie, rushing toward me and proceeding to pull me onto the pavement.

"Hannah! What's wrong with you? Do you want to get hit by a car?" Her mousy brown hair whipped around her head messily as the wind picked up.

I apologized sheepishly. "Sorry. I'll be more careful. Um, I didn't know you lived around here."

"I live in the block of apartments over there." Carrie gestured vaguely to somewhere behind her. "I saw you walking over, so I thought we could go to work together. But you suddenly turned around and stayed there for a long time." She gave me a strange look. "Were you…talking to yourself?"

"Of course not!" I replied indignantly. "I was with someone. A guy."

"What guy?" A quizzical expression formed on her face. "I didn't see anyone. What did he look like?"

"Normal. Tall, wearing a blue raincoat, had a brown bag?"

She shrugged, puzzled. "I really didn't see anyone. No offense, but it looked like you just zoned out or something. You were staring at nothing. Next time choose a safer place to space out, yeah?"

I started to become frustrated. "I told you, I was with someone. All those people must've blocked your view."

"Oh. Okay." Her disbelieving look made me feel more annoyed. She glanced at me. "Cute scarf, by the way."

~~~

Today is a special day. Today I'm going to meet him properly. I'll return his scarf and ask if he wants to get coffee.

I stand by the crossing and wait, anxiously twirling the ends of his scarf around my fingers. Seven thirty. The green walking figure appears, and crowds that have gathered on both sides of the road start to cross. I don't cross this time—I wait for him to come over.

He doesn't.
~~~

I peer over people's shoulders, trying to spot him. He had been there every single day at seven thirty without exception. But eight o'clock passes, then nine o'clock, then ten. I didn't know his phone number. I didn't even know his name. I call in sick to work and wait like the idiot that I am.

I wait until the sun sets and the sky darkens to black. The number of people and cars decrease until the only person I've seen in the last ten minutes is a drunk making his way back home. Clouds form above my head, and rain starts falling like bullets. It was like a bad Korean drama. In this story, I guess the girl and guy don't get together in the end. The girl just gets soaked to the bone by a rainstorm and may get sick later, with or without a stupid red scarf.

I got bored while waiting so I decided to count people. Today eight thousand three hundred and twenty-six people passed the crossroads in front of me. He wasn't one of them.

~~~

Sometimes, I would cross that road at seven o'clock. Sometimes seven thirty or eight. Maybe nine, ten, eleven o'clock. I never saw him again. Eventually I moved away to an apartment closer to the city center, therefore I stopped going to that place. Occasionally, the thought of him crosses my mind. I wonder if he moved away as well. I don't know why I was so drawn to him. Perhaps I wanted to live in one of my fantasy worlds. Wanted to escape from reality, wanted my knight in shining armor to take me far away from this dull place. When I think of him, I also remember Carrie's confusion from that day. As the memories of him became more distant from my mind, I wonder if he was a figment of my imagination. Someone I made up in one of the loneliest times of my life. Was I deeply infatuated with someone that was only in my head?

But the red scarf that he placed gently around my neck; I took it home with me that night. I hung it at the back of my closet. It's still there.
~~~

Mortimer

Lucy Liversidge

The day was growing old. It was the dead of winter, and war tore through the countryside like fire in a forest. Screaming souls, hundreds of last breaths, terrified soldiers distraught with the idea that this was the end—it was all just a normal day for me. I was exhausted from long hours of work and decided to lie down on the side of the road to rest.

Thousands of weary fighters passed by, beginning their journey back to the loved ones they'd left behind all those weeks ago. Far too worn out for anything but thoughts of home, none of these men suspected I would be following them back, as if they had forgotten my grasp reached far beyond the battlefields. Perhaps they had escaped for now, but we would meet again.

Just then a handsome young man grew fatigued and sat down beside me, knowing not what he was getting himself into. He peered through me to the fiery sun sinking behind the horizon, but just for a moment, it felt as if he saw my eyes. This encounter was not a coincidence, by any means. I had met this man and his family once before, and I haven't been able to forget that day ever since.

Max and his wife…what's her name? Nora, that's right. The two had just had their first child, a son, and were nothing short of overjoyed at his arrival. I guess that's what made what happened next so much harder. They were so excited and so ready to be parents. But that little boy was sick, very sick. As I descended upon the family in his last moments, I could sense his resistance. I swear he pushed me away with the last means of energy his tiny body could muster; he would've been a fighter, just like his father. His eyes shone so brightly, and I felt a twang of guilt for taking him from this world, but he wasn't ready. He just wasn't.

Oh, how Nora cried; I don't blame her. That little boy's soul felt so special in my calloused, old hands. I remember it well; their anger ran so deep, but what they didn't realize was that maybe I was doing them a favor. Maybe, just maybe, I'm not such a bad thing after all, and that their fear was only holding them back.

But that's not today's story. Today's story is me, Max, and an old, dusty road. As we sat on the side of that ravaged, blood-soaked highway, I could see the toll of the war. It showed itself in the corners of his blue eyes. They had dulled since the last time I looked into them. Now, as I searched for the source of his sullen visage in seas of glaucous, my last encounter with his family came flooding back to me. I knew what was to come for this sweet clan of three, and I knew it wasn't going to be easy, for any of us.

Darkness had suffocated the pasture as Max took his first step toward home. I had planned to part paths with him not a mile down the road. A mile turned into two, and before long, I was walking purposefully on his left. Without knowing it, Max had invited me into his home. I think it was his eyes. It took us three days. During that time, I grew close to Max. I learned of life at home in his letters: of hard times and good ones, of the evil power of death that managed to overcome the couple's first child, and of a newborn baby, a girl—but of course, I already knew all about her. Eva was one of the most beautiful children I've ever seen, and her soul was just as alluring. If I could have, I would have told him to hold her tight and shield her from the ways of the world.

As we arrived at the little cottage, just off the road, the wail of the little girl's cry pierced the forest. In an instant, I remembered the memories and swollen faces. And her eyes, they were the same eyes that looked at me with such refusal all those years ago. She had gotten them from her father. It was at that moment that I almost walked away; I almost turned around and left this family to live in peace, but I knew I had a job to do. There was no changing that.

Nora was as kind and gentle as ever, immediately welcoming her husband and ensuring he felt at home. Just think of that, a newborn child, a home to tend to, and all that matters to you is if there is plenty of food on the table and a warm bed for a war-torn soldier. That's Nora for you. I'd always seen her as the motherly type. But as I got to know this family, it became all too clear that my time with them was nothing short of essential. Over full plates and brimming glasses I listened intently as the couple recounted their journey in a kind of celebratory nostalgia. There is nothing like loss to bring people closer together.

The path had not been an easy one what with financial challenges and their struggle with the death of their son just three years ago, but I could see the overwhelming love in their eyes. "It was so hard for us to come to terms with the fact that our son, whom we waited with such high expectations and excitement for, was taken away from us just like that. Death can be such a cruel thing." And as Nora broke down in tears, I heard her mutter, "We've done nothing to deserve this. Why did this have to happen?"

I wish I could've jumped right up and said it. I wish I could have told them that I was the one that took their son from them, but that I didn't want to; I had to. I'm not as cruel as everyone thinks. There are so many days I wish I could just quit my job, but that's not a luxury I have. It's just not. The only thing I could do now is change the opinions of these two, rightfully distraught by the loss of their son.

It was four days into my stay with the family when Eva started to feel warm. Not that I wasn't expecting it, but then again, Nora's loud cry of anxiety took me by surprise. And then the strangest thing happened; even though I knew exactly what was coming next, I did just about everything I could to salvage the life of this precious little girl. We elevated her head, fed her more fluids, and bathed her tiny body in tepid water, but just as I had foreseen, nothing worked, and her fever kept rising.

As I got to know this family more intimately, it became harder and harder to stay among such saddened, charming souls. I so badly wanted to just leave them alone, but I couldn't. Why couldn't I?

About three days later, it became clear there was nothing left to do but pray. Eva's fever was rising, and our hope was declining by the moment. I could hear Nora's howls to the heavens. All she wanted was to keep her baby, anything for that baby. And when Eva's eyes closed for the last time…well, I'm not usually one to express emotion, but if I have ever felt sadness, that was it. I was expecting a struggle, perhaps refusal, but instead I was met with a smile. I swear she smiled as I grasped her beautiful soul as tenderly as I could just as the sun was breaking through the trees. It felt like a deep rose pink.

I know I will never be able to forgive myself for taking such a precious being's life, but I guess I've come to terms with that. Nora and Max are a different story. Distraught doesn't do it, and neither does agony. There truly are no words to express the sensation in the air that morning. And before I could even muster the words "I'm sorry," Nora was accusing me of bringing disease into their home, even of infecting Eva. I can't blame her though. I would probably do the same.

So the next day I packed up and left that home behind. It was probably about time; I don't think I've ever stayed in one place for so long. I felt like I had failed that family though. I knew their beloved baby girl had to come with me one way or another, but I could have at least made it easier for them. I could have at least tried to tell them I don't like my job, that this isn't easy, that they're going to be okay.

I kept checking in, but every day was the same as the one before that. Hysterical and dysfunctional, Nora and Max didn't know what to do with themselves and couldn't carry on. I wished so badly I could return to them, as a man, as Mortimer, and explain to them why death isn't such a bad thing and that the pain Eva would have had to live with would be greater than any pain they were feeling right now.

It wasn't until weeks later when they finally understood. The coroner's report had come back, and upon looking over his findings, while fighting back tears, it became clear that as much as they'd wanted Eva to remain with them in this world, she was so much better off out of it. It sounds strange, but death was a blessing for this sweet child, undeserving of the pain she would have had to bear here on Earth. I like to think that the heavens saw the tenderness in Eva's heart and could not bear to be without her for another second.

I saw Nora and Max once again, years later. The sun was just making its way out from behind the mountains on the distant horizon. I descended upon the two of them, sweeping their last breaths right out from under their wrinkled, worn bodies; it felt as if they recognized me. In fact, Nora looked right at me with those same big, blue eyes and fearlessly let her soul fall into my arms, just like that. So submissive, so willing. Max wouldn't let me near him without a struggle; he battled the heavy apparition that was my presence until his threadbare muscles had nothing left to give. And as I drifted away from that same quaint cottage all those years later, my arms full, I realized there was no one in this world I'd rather be.

Don't get me wrong. There are days when the guilt feels like it's just too much to stomach, but then I look into eyes like those of Eva's and know there is no one more qualified to help those suffering than Death himself.

Cossack Pride

Logan Egle

I snapped the bolt of my rifle into place. Pavlo, a longtime friend, shushed me as I strapped the gun to my saddle and replaced it with a six-foot lance. Along its iron tip, silvery moonlight played like a child in a river.

We had orders from the general, Pyotr Bagration, to strike the Grande Armée, which had been making its way through Russia for the last couple months. All of us here knew that we few hundred Cossacks were no match for Napoleon's Leviathan of an army, so our plan was to cut deep and run.

Alexei, our battalion leader, strode briskly about our ranks doing a last check of our gear. "Bring the cavalry just beyond that ridge. Watch close for the French and don't pounce until they're out in the open," he ordered.

I wheeled my horse around to follow the other forty. We trotted across the cold grass and hid just out of sight. Her ears perked up, and I knew she could sense my nervousness. It was hard to hide as a thin line of fearful sweat soaked the fur brim of my hat. My eyes shifted to the scars on my palms and fingers that I got from working on my father's ranch many years ago. Those days were long gone, and the more I thought about them, the more I realized how far away I was from my family and my home. Sure, war was in my blood, but unlike many, I found no joy in death and bloodshed.

To my left was Igor Sokolov. His white knuckles grasped a wooden crucifix that shook violently in his sweaty hands.

"Calm, brother," I said, trying to soothe his fear.

His voice was stuttering. "There is no calm in war…no peace. Last week when we raided the French camps, I remember the feeling of my spear crushing a man's ribs and ripping through his body. All around me were corpses. That day I saw the fires of hell and the horns of the devil on my head—"

He was cut short by the echo of a gunshot. All heads, both animal and man, turned to the direction of its source, and not a second later, countless more ripped through the silent darkness.

I looked to the scout who stood up on the ridge. "Where are they?"

"Forest's edge. Hold on a bit longer."

Another shot tore through the breezy night. The scout let out a cry, and a black, misty cloud glittered in the moonlight as he tumbled down the hill. A horn erupted among our ranks, and the war cries of men lifted up the sky around me.

I spurred my horse into a gallop and launched over the ridge. Blasts from a hundred guns rung in my ears as I charged, lowering my lance. A man in front of me stood helplessly as he tried to reload his rifle. I thrust the death-laced iron forward. A blood-curdling scream burst from his mouth, and my arm shot back on contact. I flung the dead weight from my weapon.

A bullet struck my horse in the flank, causing it to run wild. Unable to control it, my mount trampled a fellow Cossack. The horse eventually collapsed and sent me through the air.

I tumbled hard on the ground. There was a ringing in my ears and the taste of blood in my mouth. When I recovered my senses, I realized that a body of a Cossack lay before me with half of a face. The warm grass was matted down with the contents of his skull. Tears of both fear and sorrow welled up in my eyes, but the words of my father echoed in my head: "The world won't show you mercy when you need it most, so stand up, wipe the blood from your brow, and fight as your people have always fought."

I scrambled to my feet and snatched up the rifle that lay next to the dead man. My hands lined up the open sights with my eyes. I trained them on a French soldier who was taking cover behind a mound of dirt. My finger squeezed the cold trigger, and the air around me exploded as the gun punched hard against my shoulder. My eyes followed the soldier as the rifle fell from his hands and his limp body crumpled. The steaming shell jumped into the air, and I thrust the bolt back into position. To my right, a bullet thumped into the ground. Without thinking, I shot up and broke into a full sprint across the field. I hopped over fallen men and dove behind the corpse of a horse. Now that I had time to think I realized that I was facing death alone. Bodies of my friends littered the grass, and their blood turned the greenery into a dark, mottled mess.

Deep in my chest, I felt something…a fire igniting with the pride of the Cossacks as the kindling. I opened up the receiver of my rifle and loaded in another golden bullet. This was for the tsar, for my friends, for my family back home, and for Russia. Like a cannon's rip cord, my cry of war echoed in the fading night. I stood once more and aimed. One after the other, I let loose bullets, each one like a stroke of Death's blade. Blood soured the sweet breeze, and the bodies of countless Frenchmen covered the ground.

I ducked back under cover and winced every time I heard the thumping of bullets ripping into the dead horse. The last gleaming shell popped from the gun, and I fumbled around my satchel until I felt the cold metal of another magazine.

My shaking hands fumbled to load it into the rifle, but once it fell into place and I pulled out the mag pin, I realized it was too late. Savage screams sounded nearby, and a soldier dressed in dark blue vaulted over the horse. I glanced up in fear, instinctively drawing the long dagger that rested at my side. Raw muscle power launched me upward at the man. I thrust the steel blade at him, and the barrel of his pistol exploded. A searing pain spread through my whole gut as my blade cut through clothes and sunk into soft flesh. He fell to the ground, dropping his gun and clutching the wound that now soaked his dark uniform. Crimson blood dripped from my dagger. My eyes darted from the blade to the dying man. I could see the pain in his eyes, yet I saw the flag patch on his shoulder, and I remembered seeing that same flag standing high above the burning city of Smolensk.

With primordial savagery, I pounced on him and drove the dagger into his chest. Again and again, I ripped through sinew and muscle even after his heart ceased to beat.

Finally, I backed off, the blade still protruding from the Frenchman's corpse. Silence is what remained. There were no gunshots, no screams of the fallen…no thunder of the cavalry. I fell to my knees. Maybe this was what hell was like. Tales and legends told of the flames and the cackling demons, but there was only death, darkness, and despair.

A single pair of feet trod across the damp grass, and I looked up to see a man dressed in blue. The silvery light reflected a bushy mustache and a short scar that ran along his left cheek. His eye gleamed with a dull gray, and so did the cold muzzle that was aimed at my head. Tears began to stream down my face, which was stained with blood that was not mine.

"Shoot," I said. "If this is war, then I don't to be a part of it." The tears came harder now. "I just want to go home."

The Frenchman lowered the rifle and let out a shaky sigh. He may not have understood what I said, but he understood how I felt. I watched as his hand went under his bloodied coat. It produced a brass locket. The surface was scratched and faded. The man opened it and revealed a picture of him, his wife, his daughter, and two sons.

To my surprise, he spoke my language. "We are men of free will, yet sometimes we do not get to choose the life we wish to live. I hate this war as much as you do. I pray every night to God that someday I might be able to see my children and my wife. Though the light is distant, it is still there and one day it will come. But until that day comes, we must fight to hold the honor of our lost brothers, and when this is all over, we will remember the many who fought and the many who died. Napoleon thinks he can take the power from the people, but he forgets that we are men, and history tells stories of how men always rise above tyrants."

My eyes met his, and he helped me to my feet. In this silent field, us two who once wanted to kill the other stood in peace side by side.

"Hold deep in your heart the spirit of humanity and peace, but as long as the unloved rule over us, never stop fighting." The man picked up his rifle, turned toward the forest, and began to walk away. I stood there on the battlefield, alone and covered with French blood. Behind me, I heard the low beat of the hooves. Maybe they were friends? Maybe they were French? I didn't care. Everything around me was bleary, and the sound of the horses seemed to grow more and more distant until a dull, white light pushed out the death, the suffering, and the world.

Space Invaders

Daphne Bargeman

Emmett had spent a whopping three dollars now—three of the five he got on the weekends after chore day. Twelve agonizing games of Space Invaders, only for each to end in a boisterous collision of an asteroid and his unsuspecting spacecraft. He was getting frustrated now, and the smirk on Avery's face did nothing but thwart him further.

"You're a pain," he seethed at Avery, only after wasting his last quarter. He was supposed to use that quarter to let his grandmother know when he'd be home, but he was so dead set on getting past the second level (which he never did) to prove Avery wrong. "You kept distracting me."

Avery rolled her eyes. "I did nothing but tell you this was a waste of time. You're not beating my high score." She loved messing with Emmett like this, because she knew how competitive he was, that the teasing is what would lead to a combative game of pinball the following Saturday. And yes, while Emmett was the competitive type, victory wasn't the only thing that kept him coming back to The 1up every weekend. Avery didn't need to know that though.

They walked with their arms linked, breathing in the summer air, All Stars padding across the dirt road in unison. Emmett would stretch his leg out a bit too far every now and then, tripping up the girl on his right, and Avery would step out of sync for a moment, pausing a beat to get back on it. Anyone would find the sight charming, puppy love at its finest. It was cute, until they reach Avery's driveway, and

Emmett awkwardly rocked on his heels when her dad stepped out from the front porch with a scowl on his face, knuckles white from the grip he had on his box cutter.

"There's no need to be scared. The only reason my daddy carries that around is because he's scared," Avery had told Emmett one afternoon like today's, when her father sat on the porch waiting for the two to come back, a cigarette in hand and the same ugly dip between his brows.

Emmett tried to remember that when she waved goodbye to him, and her dad threateningly toyed with the switch that made the blade dip in and out of the gadget, like a snake tasting the air. It was tacky, just like Avery's father, but there wasn't a doubt in his mind that he would cut off Emmett's pinkie finger in a heartbeat.

He waited until she disappeared through the door before he spun on his heels to walk back home to his grandmother's. The menacing glare from Avery's dad didn't fail to leave a hole in the back of his baseball cap.

The sun was beginning to set by the time Emmett got home, and the smell of turkey, mashed potatoes, and green beans clouded the air. He hoped they were steamed string beans and not the ones his grandmother dumped from a can—he hated canned vegetables.

"Emmet? Is that you?" Margaret, his grandmother, called from the kitchen.

"Ma'am?"

She emerged from the foyer with a towel in her hands. "You never called to let me know when you'd be getting back. I would have started dinner a bit earlier if I had known you would be here so soon."

He shrugged and plopped on the ugly floral printed recliner that his grandmother couldn't bring herself to get rid of. It was lumpy and cold from the plastic covering she left on it. Emmett couldn't find the sense in owning furniture if it wasn't comfortable enough to sit on.

"I figured if I was home before the streetlights came on, it wouldn't matter much if I called you."

Margaret was behind the stove again now. "Still hanging out with that Wheeler girl, are you? Don't know why you're wasting your time. You know her daddy isn't too fond of you," she said.

"Well, I don't care too much what he thinks," Emmett retorted, a scoff leaving his lips. He set the table before sitting quietly across from his grandmother and eating turkey, mashed potatoes, and green beans—from a can.

It was later that night when he heard a tap on his window. He was glad his room was on the first floor, where Avery could easily slide in and out of his window for a game of Uno, sometimes even on school nights.

"We're not playing doubles! You can't do that!"

"That's a nine, not a six."

"Emmett, you know I'm actually dyslexic. That was so insensitive for you to say. You should have just let it happen."

They bicker through the night, and it's two in the morning when they finally grow bored of board games and card dealing, and talking just seems easier than leaving for Avery.

"Sorry you have to deal with all of my dad's bull," she sympathized. Her mom had told her never to use that word; it wasn't ladylike, and no boy would ever marry her if she talked like a man. She didn't care. Emmett didn't care.

"No." Emmett laughed. "I'm sorry you have to live with him. He's kind of a turd."

She laughed, like she always did with Emmett, and rolled on her side to look down the bed where he lay on the floor. Her heart fluttered when his brown eyes met her own, and she forgot what she was going to say. Their faces were oddly close. There was a weird pause, where they just looked at one another, and it might have been nice if they weren't teenagers who didn't know what to do in a situation where they had to interact with each other.

Emmett cleared his throat and sat up too quickly, and Avery backed away too slowly. Their foreheads met, and Avery shrieked too loudly.

They were both distracted by the dull ache in their skulls to notice Emmett's bedroom door crack open.

Margaret was appalled that a girl was in his bed. "Emmett Newby!"

Whiplash was all Avery could process.

Meanwhile, Emmett was well aware of the situation at hand, and just how pissed his grandmother was, and just how much more Mr. Wheeler was going to *hate* his guts.

The car ride was three minutes of agonizingly long silence. Emmett stayed back while Margaret drove Avery home. The only time Avery had ever been in the same room with Emmett's grandmother was at fifth-grade graduation, when she sat in the front row during Avery's solo of Kenny Loggins's "This is It." This was far more embarrassing.

~~~

The next week, when Avery's mom begrudgingly allowed her to leave the house to meet with that troublesome boy, Emmett Newby, things were awkward, as anticipated.
~~~

"Sorry," Emmett blurted as soon as he saw her.

She breathed out a laugh, but she was cringing, and it made Emmett do the same.

"It's fine, really. It was just weird being in the car with your grandma. Swear I saw smoke coming from her ears. Probably why it was so hot in that car." She was laughing, and she couldn't figure out why because nothing was funny, and she wanted nothing more than to curl up in a ball and disappear. "Bet she gave it to you when she came back."

Emmett was laughing too, and not only did he want to disappear, but to never come back. Their eyes were flickering back and forth nervously, until Emmett remembered where he was. He reached in his back pocket and pulled out five dollars' worth of quarters, giving ten to Avery and keeping the other half to himself. "Space Invaders?"

Avery internally gagged. "How about Super Mario Bros instead?"

Twenty quarters later and they were walking home again. Arms not linked, a respectable distance apart. They stopped in front of Avery's driveway like every Saturday, but her dad wasn't sitting on the porch as usual.

"Out of town," Avery murmured when she noticed him looking for her dad.

"Business thing?"

"Not sure."

It was quiet all of a sudden. Avery was giving Emmett the same look she had given him last week, but he couldn't run away from it this time, because he didn't want this overbearing, loud silence to go on forever between them.

Avery was kind of in her own world, and she didn't know why, but she was stepping closer to him, until the tips of their All Stars were touching.

Emmett had his chest all puffed out because he was barely breathing now, but Avery didn't seem to notice how close he was to an asthma attack.

She pecked his lips, eyes wide open. The two stared at one another before she stepped back rather fast. Emmett was choking on the words he had yet to decide on, and Avery was scratching the back of her neck. It was a nervous habit Emmett had noticed before.

She started to talk, until she sighed, gave up altogether, and breathed out a rushed "bye" before sprinting up the driveway, swinging open the front door, and disappearing until the next Saturday.

The heat in both of their cheeks could have started a fire.

The Emotional and Physical Embodiment of Stars

Maya Lewins

"Y'know, I used to love stars."

These are the first words spoken into the warm air of the bedroom in over an hour. Surprised, Eli lifts his head up from where it rested on Lane's bare chest to look at his face. His expression is unreadable, and he won't meet Eli's eyes.

"It started when I was really young. My mom told me I spent an entire day drawing constellations on my walls in Sharpie when I was four." Lane's soft chuckle vibrates through Elijah's face, ending in a vocal exhale.

"They just seemed so, I dunno, untouchable? Like, they're so distant and intangible, but then you remember that there is stardust everywhere. I think just having that assurance helped me get through a lot."

Eli didn't realize he was holding his breath until Lane had trailed off. Even after years of being together, Lane's rare moments of vulnerability still left him breathless.

"I know it's stupid," Lane mutters to his chest, and Eli wanted to cry for all the self-condemnation so evident in his voice.

Planting a sloppy kiss on his sternum, hoping to convey all the things he knows Lane wouldn't hear, Eli looks at him with something akin to devotion—and for the first time sees a myriad of stars shrouded within emerald eyes, glowing in the inky black room and incandescent with love.

Indeed, stars are everywhere.

Tracing the congregation of freckles along Lane's back a few nights later, Eli begins to make out dozens of constellations in the feeble light of daybreak. The emergence of sunrays from a nearby window cast a faint pink glow on Lane's skin, and Elijah imagines it as an interstellar cloud, enveloping these galaxies, protecting them. Lane shimmies back to lay flush against him, and stars explode where their bodies come in contact. Reveling in this newfound feeling, Eli falls asleep, fingers still lightly grazing Lane's shoulders.

"Do you still love stars?"

Lane turns to him in the small diner, the light from a nearby window highlighting impossibly emerald irises, and Elijah can almost see the billions of stardust fragments that piece him together. There is a fire beneath it all, a fervent conflagration that beams through freckle-shaped rifts along the bridge of his nose. It pulsates with strength, even when in pain, and Eli can only stare in awe. He doesn't respond, only reaches across the small table and grasps Eli's hand before bringing it up to his lips, and his fingers tingle with the residual heat of innumerable galaxies of stars.

Stars become an overwhelming constant in Eli's life. In all the spaces between him and Lane, they ignite with untapped passion and a gravitational pull of their own. They kindle with centuries of untold stories of devotion and sing songs of love that echo as a constant whisper through Elijah's mind. This new awareness engulfs him, leaves him gasping for breath.

Heat and fire burns through the oxygen and oblivion that once surrounded him. At times, there is nothing but blinding luminescence in swirling shades of amber and teal. His vision blanks, and he is left vertiginous and faint. The cool night air of their rooftop becomes his haven, a stark contrast to the sweltering conditions he never even realized he was living in.

Here, memories and visualizations of his and Lane's relationship can swirl around him, and he can pause to examine them before they are consumed by flames. Breathing deeply, he welcomes the cleansing chill of autumn air and lets his eyes drift shut.

Beneath him, he feels the dull thud of children's feet reverberate through his body, followed by high-pitched, wholesome laughter. He hears the twin creaking of rocking chairs as wrinkled and tired hands seek each other, and he sees stars deteriorating where their fingers connect.

Drawn back to reality, he feels the weight of someone approaching and looks over to see his love perched beside him. His silhouette is defined by nearby streetlights and stars that erupt to life around him, beautiful in a way he once thought impossible. Following Lane's eye line where it is fixated above his head, he is greeted by trillions of years' worth of light and hope, cascaded across the sky in waves of constellations and veils of galaxies. They demand nothing, rather supply indefinite support and comfort. They are fear and animosity, joy and ambition and love and things that Elijah couldn't and may never understand. Overcome with emotion, he looks to Lane, whose eyes remain cemented upward, an expression comparable to longing splayed across his face. He looks to Eli, and the expression unwaveringly remains. Elijah's eyes glaze over with saltwater and stardust, and when he collides his lips with Lane's, these tears birth new creations of light, bursting where soft flesh comes together. They are alive and aflame, but no longer frightening.

Crisp autumn air subdues the heat, envelopes it, leaves him breathless with desire. It is such a raw and human need, and as stars die around them, Elijah submits to it without hesitance.

The Battle That Changed Us

Charlotte Menke

We fall into a rhythmic march, our blood-ridden feet kicking up dust. Behind me, the Rappahannock River is a mere sliver twinkling below the horizon. Thousands of miles we've traveled to arrive in this foreign land, filled to the brim with Yankees. I've lost count of the days, but it's rumored we'll reach our destination by the fifteenth of June. Whispered under the breath of limping boys in rags is word that our three corps will meet not in Harrisburg, but Cashtown.

We march on.

And I, with my secret.

Past the orchards along Old Chambersburg Pike, a brick building marked Cashtown Inn comes into view. Curiosity urges my weary legs onward.

Left…right…left…right. The clanking of bayonets overrides the whelps of soldiers fighting tar heels.

General Pettigrew hollers, "Keep movin' boys. We're gettin' shoes in Gettysburg."

My feet cannot handle nine more miles. The back of my neck, once covered by long locks, cannot handle more sunburn. Yet I carry on.

The next day, I awake to the red, white, and blue of our flag peeking out from behind the mist. The rumble of hooves is faint, but I know the Union Army is here.

But we wait for the command from the men aptly dressed, with gleaming buttons, aboard stallions.

An elbow finds my rib cage, the grinning soldier displaying his few teeth like prized cattle. Toothless is overeager to fight, but I, who have actual warfare knowledge, worry about the delay.

I may be a woman. But I am not naive.

My craving for danger led me here, just like the men. If we must fight, we'll fight converged. We need a strong defensive stand on high ground. I smile, for I might be more educated on tactics than half the soldiers in front of me.

"Frank!" Matthew hands me a letter.

My cheeks burn with my secret. If Matthew hadn't covered me in our last battle, while I reloaded my rifle, I wouldn't be here today. I owe him the truth, but…would he turn me in? I take the letter. Before ripping open the seal, we're ordered to move out.

Left…right…left…right. My heart races, a ticking bomb. If I get wounded, my cover'll be blown. Please, Lord, do not send me home. I'd rather die than weep on the doorstep, a broom in hand.

"FIRE!" Our soldiers turn into savages on the Union.

Using my teeth, I tear open my paper powder cartridge and with shaking fingers place the minié ball into the rifle's barrel. My percussion cap sparks, and a wicked shot soars.

General Archer arrives with two brigades.

Reload, one minute.

Twenty seconds, *bam*, shoot. Reload, one minute.

Twenty seconds, *bam*, another whistling bullet.

My hands work deftly until a roan gallops through our line blanketed with Union General Reynolds's limp body.

Jason could share this fate.

We advance farther. Our lines seem to stretch on for miles—the mismatched uniforms in shades of gray. Our lines are compressed by a Union flank attack, but in the midst of this, the boys whisper and point at the Union.

A salient! A mistake in their lines.

"Forward, boys! Give it all ya got!" Pettigrew belts.

Underneath my musket is a long-time friend, my bayonet. Howls and thumps of falling bodies surround me. At last, the line is broken, and the Union scrambles in retreat toward Gettysburg. Ewell's officers scream, "We must take the hill!"

If Stonewall were here, we'd be halfway up the hill already. The sky wraps us in a chilled blanket of milky stars. My muscles ache, and I cringe over the rotting flesh.

Back at the tent, I quickly undress while the boys bathe in a stream. To think I'd feared the physical exam. Recruiters were eager for able bodies, as long as they had fingers to pull the trigger and two teeth to open a powder packet. Few young men can even grow a beard, allowing my rosy, feminine cheeks to blend in. Yet I worried they'd spit at me in disgust, claiming a woman was a waste. Why did I want the job? War was thrilling and mysterious—and thirteen dollars was better than any pay a woman could get.

I sigh, opening this morning's letter.

> *Dear Sister,*
>
> *I heard you enlisted for the Confederate Army. You're a disgrace to the family. Just imagine, Ma and Pa blushin' with embarrassment when asked about you, the harsh stares on the streets. No man'll marry a battle-scarred hooligan. Shame'll be brought upon our name. I don't think I shall ever call you sister again. I'm begging you to return home, save yourself from the horrors of battle and save your southern bell reputation. My corps will be defending hard tomorrow, and Sykes'll have us pound down Confederate corps until our last breaths. It's obvious to me that Meade's optimistic about our positions. With almost 200,000 more men and our high defensive position, this battle is ours. And even in my fury, I'd hate to see you ever meet a bullet.*
>
> *Respectfully,*
>
> *Jason*

I wipe away a tear. Was I wrong to come? Back home they'd hear no word of my service. I rip up the letter. I won't write back to Jason. Maybe my actions can prove my authority. Then I pause. If the Union's plan is to fight on the defense, the only way to break through the thick lines stacked with men will be during their weakest moment. Where is the most critical piece of Union territory?

Then it hits me.

Little Round Top.

The next day, overcast skies send shivers down my spine. Matthew sets out for pork and dark coffee. As I fasten my uniform buttons, I think of the wounded, reaching out with letters of their last words.

There's no returning now, not if we're pursued through the mountains, leading to the downfall of the supplies train. Our sergeant announces our squad and others will move out with Longstreet's men to deliver the knockout punch to the Union's left. My squad will be operating under the command of Major General John Bell Hood.

It takes hours to reach our destination. As we approach Devil's Den, I look to our Confederate flag for reassurance. The white stars shine brightly against the deep navy they rest upon.

The familiar drums cause me to ready my rifle. I look to Matthew, give him a nod. War cries boom, and Union men spring out.

Reload, one minute.

Twenty seconds, *bam*, shoot. Reload, one minute.

Twenty seconds, *bam*.

"Keep 'em coming, boys!" Hood yells.

The bayonet stabbing begins. The Union pushes off the boulders, and we regroup in preparation to reach our second destination. *Little Round Top*. There stands the grand hill—steep, rocky, overgrown. But no Union.

I gasp when I see General Hood's body down, motionless.

Our best chance is to charge the hill—now—as there are no soldiers in sight. Before I change my mind to lead the charge, my feet fly.

"Hold to the last!" I scream. "We will prevail!"

"You heard Frank, forward!" Matthew bellows.

A regiment of men follow my lead, their heads bobbing up and down as the mob increases their pace to follow me. With each step, my legs propel me faster.

The Union appears, jaws hanging at the sight of us, but artillery firing regardless.

The merciless combat begins, swords slashing and rifles shooting. More soldiers charge from the base of the hill, surprising the Union once again with a flank attack.

At the top of the hill, the Union reverts to bayonets.

I can't contain my excitement—their ammo must be gone!

I swerve my head to the side, but too late a bullet penetrates my gut.

~~~

Anniversary of Gettysburg
July 2, 1888

Twenty-five years ago, Dawn Evans proudly led the final charge of Gettysburg, a battle that changed the course of the Civil War and led the Confederate States of America to a victory. What an honor, to hear of Dawn's promotion after her heroic actions and the campaigns following, and to see her serve as a general during the final battle where she captured the Union Army's capital.

With a heavy heart, she was discharged dishonorably for serving as a woman.

Dawn proved us wrong. If anyone could've done it, it would've been her. With assistance from the press, we rallied and spread hope that social barriers could be broken. The army cannot claim no women served in the Civil War.

She was living proof.

With every detail of the war, her name will be printed in bold. When our grandchildren look back on the past, they can read about the daring southern belle, the woman who changed the course of history.
~~~

Today, we celebrate the life not of Frank Johnston but of Dawn Evans, a war hero, a darling wife, loving mother, and the one whom I have the privilege of calling my dearest sister.

Respectfully,
Jason Evans

Of Memories and Feathers

Khloe Beutler

She was the splatter of red in a black and white image, the contrast of a yellow balloon against a cloudy sky. She was the ray of sunshine on the stormiest day…and she was late.

Technically speaking, late wasn't the most reasonable term. They hadn't exactly settled on a time to meet, but Everett waited at the top of Olive Hill for hours. It was their favorite spot. Goose bumps formed on his arms as he paced restlessly against the soggy, unkempt grass. The air had a slight chill to it, despite the warm sun rays that enveloped the earth in a glow.

After accepting that he might be waiting for at least another half hour, Everett collapsed on the ground with his chin in his hands.

"And, for probably the seventeenth time today, Everett Elliot Richardson sits down in the grass, which is still wet. He once again ignores the water seeping through his pants."

Everett gave Hallie a fake glare, then burst into laughter. He loved the way she narrated people's lives. It made him feel important, like a character out of a storybook.

Hallie's face glowed in the sunlight. Freckles formed constellations on her face. She was as radiant as the sun and bold as the stars in a dark night sky.

"I don't know what I'm going to do without you," Everett confessed. This would be their last day together before Hallie moved away.

Everett tried not to think about Hallie leaving; the very thought sent tears to his eyes. Life without Hallie would be dull and colorless, and he didn't want any part of it. In a black and white picture, she could be seen a mile away with her vibrancy alone.

"Oh, get over it." Though she sounded insensitive, Everett was sure he saw the faint glimmer of a tear in Hallie's eye.

The light blue afternoon was fading into a bright orange evening. Sunsets like these were Everett's favorite. The vivid sky reminded him of Hallie's frayed ribbon curls. Everett was slightly envious of her curls. They smelled like the summer sky and a box of crayons…everything lovely.

"Oh!" Hallie bounced. "I have something to give to you!"

She started down the hill as Everett followed closely behind.

Loud giggles escaped Hallie's throat, and Everett wondered how she was capable of laughing at all. His lungs felt constricted. He was only capable of taking breaths in short, sharp intervals. His muscles tensed up, and he desperately wanted to rest.

Then Everett looked at Hallie. She was as graceful as a bird dancing through the air. A smile like no other was plastered against her face. Her arms were thrown to the side as she surrendered herself to the blazing sky.

At the sight of Hallie, Everett began to feel light. He no longer felt weighed down and even chuckled slightly himself. He did just as Hallie did, letting his arms go free. They soared through the air.

A bit of Hallie's color was beginning to rub off onto Everett. He felt it in his chest, and it warmly spread throughout his entire body.

When they reached Hallie's house, she led Everett to the back. "I'll be right back," she promised.

As he waited, Everett tried to recall all of the little things about his life with Hallie that he might forget after she moved. He thought of the way her laugh bubbled, brightening an entire room. He thought of the pattern etched into the wood of her dinner table that resembled a gnome. Everett always chose that seat so he could admire it.

Everett remembered the time he and Hallie discovered each of the squeaky sounds in the staircase. They made sure to jump on each one of them and laughed when it irritated Hallie's father. He couldn't handle having his Sunday night football interrupted.

No matter the distance between them, these were the memories Everett knew he would never forget.

"E?"

Everett turned around. Hallie's skinny, freckly arms held a box. It was covered in wrapping paper dotted with shamrocks. Big, bold letters read: "Happy St. Patrick's Day!" Hallie's mother bought wrapping paper for even the most overshadowed holidays.

It took a while to break the tape free from the cardboard. Hallie even giggled slightly as she watched him struggle. After a couple of moments, Everett pulled the fold upward and looked inside of the box. He gasped, removing the contents.

Hallie and Everett had spent a lot of time during the past years collecting feathers. It was one of the many hobbies they shared. They went on feather hunts nearly every day. Even when he found the most incredible feathers, Everett always gave them to Hallie to keep in her collection. And there it was, sitting on his lap. It was a jar full of past years spent together…of memories and feathers.

Hallie was the light in Everett's life. She was the bouquet of roses thrown at the end of a ballet performance. She was the syrup at the bottom of a mug of cocoa. She was beautiful through her curves and her edges, and all of her wonderful imperfections.

Everett struggled with the thought of how much he would miss her. But through it all, he knew the ending of this time with Hallie was only the beginning of another story. Hallie left muddy footprints in his life. They were like the ones her mother yelled at her for after she ran outside barefoot for hours. She splattered her color in Everett's life like paint.

Though it would be hard without her, Everett knew he would never forget the times he shared with Hallie. Time spent laughing over glasses of lemonade too cold to be held.

Time spent watching baking soda volcanoes overflow onto the kitchen floor. Time spent crying over all of the dogs in the city pound that might never be adopted. The good times, the bad times, and all of the times in between.

Hallie was a dreamer, a poet. Her words formed beautiful wings, and Everett watched her fly away.

Monster

Rhys Owen

Part 1: Insane

Do insane people realize that they're insane? Do they notice when they start going crazy? Or are they oblivious to everything—their thoughts, their feelings, their actions, changing, metamorphosing into something until they are completely unrecognizable?

I don't believe I'm sane, at least not in the conventional sense. But convention has never been the guideline for me.

I feel an overwhelming amount of hate growing inside me, festering, building, intensifying, although I am not entirely sure who or what the hate is for. I hate myself, for allowing me to be repressed for so long. I hate the people of my town, for rejecting me, disowning me, treating me like some kind of monster. I hate society, for the bad joke that is its rules and morals. Their code of acceptance, of compassion, of justice dropped at the first sign of trouble. Whenever things take a turn for the worse, these civilized, *respectable* people will turn into savages. They will eat each other alive.

See, I'm not the monster here. I'm just ahead of the curve.

I stare at the neat array of weapons laid out in front of me in a tidy row, cataloged and ordered impeccably. Long ago, when the doctor diagnosed me, I was told that I was OCD. Among other things.

Carefully, I select a Walther LR300 semi-automatic assault rifle from the assortment of armaments, opening the magazine to find it fully loaded. *This one will do. This one will serve its purpose.* Machiavelli proposed an interesting choice. Whether to be feared or to be loved. I lost the ability to love long ago. Today I practice fear.

I walk out of my house into the town I so despise. My grip on the gun tightens. I stride toward a man and a woman sitting together, rage pulsating in my veins. The woman notices the gun first. Her hands drift up to her mouth, and she starts screaming. My finger travels to the trigger, and in an instant, she keels over, a bullet wound piercing her head. The screaming stops.

The man's face congeals with rage, and he charges toward me like a rabid dog. I fire once. The round hits the man in his left elbow, puncturing it in the joint, sending a visible shock wave through his body as his nerves register the pain. He lets forth a guttural scream and keeps charging forward. How could that round not stop the man immediately? The shock from that blast would surely incapacitate any human. I fire a second time, hitting the man in the chest. The force of the round knocks the man off his feet, yet he is still not dead. I shoot him a third time, this time in the head. He ceases to move any longer.

And there, splattered on the ground, instead of blood, a thick slimy liquid pours from the man onto the hard, cold bitumen. The same runny fluid streams out of the woman too. I blink uncomprehendingly at the vile stuff as it oozes out of the corpses' gaping wounds, leaving a trail of bright green streaks on the midnight-black tarmac.

Somewhere, through the fog of hatred in my mind, it clicks. On this day, my fellow townspeople have turned into zombies. I see that now. My killing is justified, and I am happy to continue my rampage, a new energy entering my system.

My vision blurs, and I resume the purge, renewed by glorious purpose. Rage blocks all clarity of mind. Walking through the town, I must have now killed hundreds of zombies. Their dead bodies are strewn behind me, the slime-blood bursting forth from each of their mangled corpses. It seems as if I've done it. It seems as if I have killed them all. If anyone was still alive, I would be considered a hero. If they saw what I was doing, how I saved the world, I would be famous. I would be noticed. And maybe loved.

I sink to my knees, letting out a maniacal laugh. I have succeeded. I am a savior; I have saved them all. I hear sirens in the distance and men shouting, coming for me. Rough hands grab me, handcuff me, haul me away, but I don't care. I am filled with a pleasure, a happiness the doctor told me I was incapable of feeling. How very wrong was he. Perhaps he would see his mistake if he were still alive.

The descent into madness is like a fall from a cliff; the impact is not in the fall, but the landing.

I have landed, and now my mark is made.

Part 2: Trial

The crowd in the courtroom is composed of all types—from journalists to grieving families to intrigued medical professionals to the simply curious. They collectively hold their breath as the wild-haired man is led in chains to the far-left side of the bench and seated there. The seat beside him is vacant, but the two seats next to that are filled by two grim-faced prosecutors.

The shooting was well publicized for both its heinousness and its magnitude. The defendant's ridiculous "not guilty" plea only added fuel to the fire. There are whispers, whispers of his madness, of ravings of zombies and slime-blood and impossible things. But no insanity plea was made, and no doctor was brave enough to wade against the torrent of media-fueled hate to make a contradictory diagnosis.

Justice indeed.

The eyes of the crowd, some moist with tears, some narrowed with hatred, some wide with interest, watch the defendant for any sign of fear as he waits for his fate to be decided in a murder trial without a defense. They are disappointed.

"Monster!"

A voice rings out from the throng of muttering spectators, a loud voice, filled with pain and loathing, a voice that breaks as it releases the word from hollowed, sunken cheeks. More join the cry, as if attempting to avenge their lost family and friends, but they falter at the lack of reaction from their target. Instead they content themselves with silent, rage-filled gazes.

The judge waits for the commotion to die down and begins the trial.

If there wasn't ample anger and hatred in the room to begin with, each testimony, each witness, each sentence from the prosecutors exacerbates these feelings until the crowd, even the curious and uninvested, are at fever pitch. It exceeds boiling point after merely the first few testimonies and continues to increase, outrage and a desire for justice swelling in proportion with the case against the defendant.

When some of the less gruesome surveillance footage is shown, some among the crowd even start threatening to do their own sort of justice to the defendant.

Throughout the proceedings, while the evidence, the condemnation, and the loathing building against him, the defendant never changes his empty, cold, detached expression. When the final witness sits down—a sobbing widow and childless mother—a stunned silence falls over the courtroom. The sea of eyes shift to stare as if for the first time at the perpetrator.

Looking for what, they are unsure. Remorse? Regret? Sorrow? Perhaps even just the slightest reaction to what they had heard.

And then, shockingly, he smiles, sneers, a mocking smile, goading, snapping them out of their stupor.

Uproar.

The crowd begins shouting. A single word. An ugly word. A bloodthirsty word. The chant echoes throughout the chamber, loud and insistent, the people passing their sentence.

The gavel bangs three times. The crowd falls silent, but the ghost of the word, that fateful word, hangs in the air as if urging the judge on. Insistent. Bloodthirsty. Savage.

The judge glances around and sees tears, pain, hate. And then, a grim expression worn on his face, he gives the verdict.

Part 3: Sentence

It is an indictment on society that this is how one who is nothing less than a savior is treated. It would almost shock me had I not seen it before, the way they treat their heroes like villains. And I am, undoubtedly, the former; after all that town had done to me, how it wronged me, I still mustered the benevolence to save it from its impending disaster, though I could've walked away and left it to the zombie threat.

And for this heroic deed how am I rewarded?

I am roughly seized and handcuffed, handled with misguided *contempt* rather than reverence, brought to court, tried and flushed down the "justice" system before being spat out here, to the place where society plunks all those who don't conform with their twisted imitation of morality.

Death row.

Justice indeed.

I'm not afraid to die; at least that's what I tell myself. If I was afraid to die, I wouldn't have risked my life defending my reviled town from the zombie assault. No, I do not fear death. My hands are shaking for some other reason. Anger, perhaps? Yes. Anger. At the situation, at the injustice. Not fear. Anger.

The needle looks like any other ordinary innocent needle, the kind a doctor would use to inject a vaccine. But this needle is no vaccine; this needle holds death in its barrel, bestowing it as indiscriminately as the barrel of my gun.

Only this time it's me waiting for death to arrive.

My eyes track the needle as it's raised and then plunged down in a deadly arc, heading for my exposed skin.

I close my eyes waiting for the inevitable to follow.

Contact. Penetration. Then only darkness.

Blu Birdie

Jordan Nelson

Sweet air trickles past my face as my feet kiss the land I so long to be away from. Whenever I manage to pull away from the force that keeps me grounded, and I spread my fingers to the blue expanse of wind, my feet always return to their lover. So as I glide through the vast wheat fields of the south, my speckled-robin-egg eyes stare sharply at the figure in the distance. Higher and higher it soars—the bird.

Fragile heart beating.

Lungs expanding.

Muscles moving.

I reach out as if to touch its soft exterior and feel its feathers brush over my hand. But alas, I am one with the ground, and it is a child of the sky.

Standing somberly at the edge of the field behind the fence of sodden wood, I yearn to climb its planks and take off running on the other side. To let the wind carry me away on its airy breeze. Farther and farther. I let my hand linger on the wood for just a second longer before pulling it away in a hurry and turning around. I walk slowly, feet dragging in the dirt, humming the song of the wind and drawing pictures in the air. My arms are sore by the time I reach the town where I live but do not call home. My pale yellow dress is stained with grass, and I hang my head low to ignore the piercing looks of the folks who think themselves above outside play.

I stopped caring about the way their heads dip down and how a shadow falls over their eyes when they meet mine. I keep my gaze cast upon the ground and my shoulders squared back as I walk to the house I inhabit with my mother and nana. Like the birds, I am a free soul, and I don't need people's input on how to live my life.

After slowly pulling open the old iron fence gate, I cringe at the sharp whine it makes as I close it carefully. After heading around to the back of the house, I use the garden hose to scrape the grime off my hands and shoes.

"Birdie? Birdie, is that you, dear?"

I nod and realize that she can't see my face. I call out yes, and my mother unlatches the back door, singing a sweet melody under her breath. She pulls me into a warm embrace, before pushing me back and holding me at arm's length. After looking me over, she wrinkles her nose in disgust. I smile sheepishly at my dirty state. She shakes her head and runs her hands through her dusty blonde hair. Then she points upstairs with a silent meaning of getting changed.

After running up the creaky wooden stairs, I pass my nana's room and poke my head in.

"Nana? Are you awake?"

The old lady coughs twice before opening her tired chocolate eyes. She looks at me for a second before smiling softly.

"I am now, sweetheart."

I look down, but she just chuckles.

"It's all right, my dear Bird. You look tired. Why not rest for a while with Nana?" Her coughing fit starts up again, and I back away. Her eyes seem troubled as I quickly explain my mother's orders. I ask for dismissal, and she smiles, nodding ever so slightly. I walk at a slow pace, worn out from the sadness that overwhelms me. Her sickness has been getting worse, and we just don't have the money to treat it. Nana has always been there, even when my mother was not. She's been my second mother for my entire life, and the fact of her sickness causing her pain fills my eyes with tears that threaten to fall over.

After shrugging on my light blue dress, I backtrack down the stairs, carefully avoiding my nana's doorway. I end up sitting at the dinner table staring at the empty place setting that will never be filled again. My father used to shuffle into the kitchen quietly and grab my mother around her waist, lifting her up to twirl her around. I remember the smile that used to spread over her face like fresh jelly. I don't see that smile anymore. I haven't seen it since Father visited the birds.

Dinner goes as it usually does—silent and undisturbed. I used to watch my mother's movements, but she has started building up her wall again. Brick by brick, she walls herself in. Oblivious to the life that's beginning to unravel around her. Oblivious to her growing daughter who isn't interested in boys and fancy clothes. The daughter who just wants to be free.

I quietly clean up the table while my mother stares vacantly at the chair from which my father would sit. She nods numbly at my request to leave for a while, and I tread quickly down the garden path and out the gate. I'm sprinting down the partly paved road before I can even comprehend where I'm going to go. Tears are trailing silently down my face making my vision blur and my pace slow. I hit someone almost immediately and fall down onto my back.

"Hey, watch it!"

I scramble up, muttering apologies.

Before I can finish, the boy says, "Oh, oh, it's just you Birdie. Are—are you okay?"

My head drops, and my cheeks redden at the instant pity that has formed on the boy's tongue.

"I'm fine," I say softly. I keep saying that phrase until I don't believe it anymore.

I walk home, repeating the friendly words my nana always tells me to recite when the birds fly away.

"Don't get blue, Bird. You'll get another chance to see them. Stay, my sunshine." And with a chime of her singsong laugh, she'd repeat it even quieter. "Don't get blue, Birdie."

Her voice in my head makes me laugh, and her words rattle around in my head. I remember writing them down once. I forgot the *e* in *blue*. But Nana still smiled and hung it up on her wall. My mother tore it down two days later. She said only pretty things deserve to be making holes in the walls that are already filled with holes. But Nana just winked at me and placed it under her bed frame, whispering that it would bring the birds and convince them to watch over us.

When my mother comes tearing down the street screaming my name, tears dripping from her eyes, I'm not so sure the birds are watching over us.

After wildly grabbing my shoulders and sobbing words of gibberish, she holds my arm tight and drags me home ignoring my frantic questioning. She collapses on her knees once we enter the door frame of the front door and points upstairs, her arm shaking madly. I run upstairs, fearing the worst, and a feeling of sickness rushes through my body when I see my nana taking some of her last breaths. Buckets of tears pour out of my eyes as I slide to the ground and take her hand in my own. With her last remaining efforts, she mumbles the words, "Don't.... get..." Her coughing fit starts up again, but her warm eyes find mine. She smiles one last time, before I watch the life flood out of her face. I look down, still crying wildly, and say the last word:

"Blue..."

I don't talk to my mother for days. I have nothing to say to her.

I mostly sit in the wheat field and stare at the fence.

I was so close to it once. Practically dancing on the other side.

But now it's miles away.

Cold air pushes past my face as my feet drag tiredly against the mounds of dirt. Through sleep I manage to escape the world that doesn't belong to me anymore. So as I stomp through the old wheat fields of the south, my dark eyes stare blankly at the figure in the distance. Lower and lower it descends—the bird.

Fragile heart stopping.

Lungs contracting.

Muscles tightening.

I reach out as if to touch its cold body and feel its feathers once more before they turn to dust. But alas, I am one with the living, and it is one with the dead.

I tell the bird to say hello to my nana, before turning my back and walking away.

Unplayed Duet

Arunima Jaiswal

Somewhere where the stars sing and burn bright, a picture falls down. The boy in the picture is eaten away by flames.

Somewhere where the stars are simply legends, tales told through generations, a girl's world is about to be completely shattered.

Amie sat on the railing of her porch, watching the chimes sing while her brother, Caleb, harmonized with the rich tones of his viola. Amie knew she was too old to be doing nothing with her time, when there were chores to be completed and a home to maintain, but she allowed herself the opportunity to close her eyes and lose herself in the music.

Somewhere between the singing stars and the harsh ground of reality, an angel cloaked in white flew, defying gravity, as she made her way to her destination.

The music halted abruptly as Caleb began to cough. Amie gazed in terror as his viola clattered to the ground with a sickening clank. Caleb's eyes were unfocused as he clutched his chest.

Somewhere where the stars were simply fantasies, a sister tried to save a lost soul, but was unable to. The angel was there, and that meant that it was too late.

"Caleb!" Amie screamed, unable to help him as the angel appeared in front of her eyes. Amie's eyes widened with shock as she comprehended the situation.

The angel. She was a rumor, a whispered tale. She was said to wear a white cloak and to have forest-green eyes with fiery crimson hair. She was one of many angels that ruled from the stars. The angels supposedly specialized in one thing, whether it be life, prosperity, or something else.

Caleb blinked blearily, noticing the angel. His expressions switched from pain, confusion, terror, and understanding all in the span of a few seconds.

"Amie," he whispered, voice hoarse, "Amethyst. I love you."

"No," Amie muttered, as she realized the gravity of the situation. "NO!"

The angel cloaked in white specialized in death.

Amie turned to the angel, shaking with fury.

"You can't just take him from me!" she shrieked.

The angel's voice was steely calm when she responded. "He has fallen in the Stelemites. He must fall on Earth."

"My brother is the only family I have left!" Amie screamed again, desperation seeping into her voice.

"Amie, please," Caleb pleaded, face contorting in pain. "Don't argue with the Angel of Death. You'll only make things worse."

"She's taking you from me," Amie replied sharply. "I can't let her do that."

Death quirked an eyebrow, intrigued.

"Such defiance…I haven't seen anything so powerful in centuries."

"I'm not a *thing*," Amie snarled before turning to Caleb and softening. "I love you, Caleb."

"I l-love you too," Caleb choked, voice deteriorating as he coughed violently. "Stay strong for me, okay?"

Amie could only nod, tears tracking down her face as Caleb faded away. Death watched Amie curiously.

"You have power," Death murmured. "Incredible power."

Sometimes, humans dreamed of what the Stelemites, or where the angels lived, was like. Some feared that the Stelemites were a ghastly cavern, with acicular stalagmites. Others fantasized that it was a heaven, with fluffy clouds and rosy skies. There were select humans who were taken to the Stelemites for their powers, but none of them ever returned.

Amie scanned her surroundings. She heard a ghostly melody and stared at the inky black sky dotted with burning stars.

She realized where she was but refused to believe it. *It isn't true. It doesn't make sense,* her mind supplied as viable reasons to ignore reality. *You're not dead.*

But before she could stop her mind from continuing, she had already thought, *Like Caleb.*

The tears fell, filled with hatred at the world.

"It helps if you move on."

It was the angel, regally looking down as she pityingly stared at Amie.

Amie felt a flare of anger as she lost control of her emotions.

"You? The reaper cloaked in white? The one who is known for taking loved ones from people? You've never felt anything like us *humans,* the feeling of losing somebody. You don't have the right to tell me to simply 'move on.'"

"I understand that you're upset," Death responded, unaffected, "but you have to understand that I had no choice. It's all fated. The Pendulant Pictures are real."

"*The* Pendulant Pictures?"

Images of burning pictures flashed through Amie's mind, and she flinched.

"Yes." Noticing Amie's reaction, Death corrected herself. "The actuality isn't as gruesome as the tales told by humans. The Pendulant Pictures exist for all of humanity; each represents an individual's life. So once a person's Pendulant

Picture is destroyed, I have to collect the corresponding soul."

Amie stood, frozen as she comprehended Death's explanation. "That's…stupid. How could someone's life be decided like that?"

Death nodded. "I sympathize. In fact…" She hesitated as she unearthed thousands of heartbreaking memories that she had suppressed. "I know how it feels to lose somebody you love."

"Please," Amie retorted, all previous shock forgotten as she regained her anger, "I doubt the pain an immortal angel would have suffered through, but at least try to explain it to me. Correct me and show me you can even *somewhat* relate."

Death pressed her lips together as part of herself regretted mentioning anything to Amie, while the other part of her knew that she must know the truth in order to trust her.

When humans are confused and lost, they tend to react in different ways. Some act kindly while others lose all sense of rationality. In the end, everybody is looking for one thing: trust. And to trust somebody, different people need different things. Some people need the truth while others need answers.

So Death took the risk and decided to tell Amie the truth. After all, Death had taken her to the Stelemites.

"I don't usually tell people this," Death warned, "for personal reasons. When you first started asking questions, I tried suppressing the memories, but I know I must tell the truth now. We…weren't meant to be. A human and something as supernatural as I. I'm not sure how it even happened, honestly. Just—his compassionate and cheerful nature. He shone innocent happiness into my dreary life of the shadows. If an angel of irony existed…"

Love and heartbreak, like all other emotions, are intangible. To describe these are impossible; even the best poets can only scratch the surface of these indescribable sensations. And even Death, an immortal deity, finds herself unable to describe her lover and crushed heart.

Death's voice broke as she relived her lost love.

"I had to take his life. Once someone's Pendulant Picture is destroyed, there are no exceptions. Even I, Death, as seemingly unbreachable as I am, have to follow the rules." She smiled bitterly. "I was as unhappy as you are, but I learned to move on. That he—he was gone forever."

Amie swallowed, taking time to organize her emotions.

She thought of her pain for Caleb. She thought of her fury when Death took him and how she had seemed so haughty when saying, "It helps if you move on." She thought of how determined she was to hate Death, the angel who stole the last of her family away from her, yet she felt undeniable sorrow and empathy as Death wove her tale of love and loss.

Amie took a shaky breath and tried to respond to Death without any anger and despair clouding her mind.

"But moving on…is so painful. And it's only been *hours*."

Death's face flashed with realization.

"I…these things take time, but it's better to start sooner, rather than later."

It hurt Amie, but she understood the logic behind Death's words.

"I guess." She wanted to add more about Caleb but felt that she couldn't say anything about him without breaking.

"Take your time and move on however will work best for you," Death responded after a moment of silence. "And, Amie? You may not be curious about this right now, but I want you to know that I did not bring you to the Stelemites simply because of your power. I brought you here because in my eyes, your true strengths lie in your emotions. Never stop being an ardent person for what and who you love, for anybody or anything."

Humanity has learned that "moving on" doesn't happen in one day or one night. It takes patience. To cope with the emotional pain, many people turn to music to create something beauteous.

In the land of endless stars and sky, Amie fiddled with the fine-tuners of her cello as she took a deep breath. *This is for Caleb,* she thought, *and the duet we never played.*

And she let the bow fly, the music gliding off the page and becoming something tangible.

Somewhere, where the stars danced among the skies, a young soul learned to accept. This soul played songs about love and played songs about death, but always played passionately.

Shadow Sister

Xuan Xuan (Angelina) Li

I imagine our sisterhood as a photograph, she the vivid foreground and I the invisible background. My twin sister stands out among the picturesque scenery and the seamless blend of filters, allowing her everyday moments to be captured by a perfect, photogenic angle. I take my place in her shadows, her multicolored life contrasting against my poor imitation in plaintive gray.

From an early age, my sister established that she was special, while I found myself to be unbearably ordinary. My first realization occurred at a childhood talent show, where I experienced a sharp stab of jealousy. I remember the dazzling spotlight trained on my sister, whose delicate voice drew an impressed hush over the crowd. I stood fidgeting in the darkness beside her, awkwardly trying in vain to rob her of the attention. My insecurities consumed me like my sister's shadows, and I wondered if I could ever step into her light.

My sister has always been pure, gratifying in the guileless way of sunshine and starlight. I am the gloomy, perplexing, troubled canvas. I am the moody rain that makes everyone cherish the warmth of her sun. My sister is admired by her peers and adored by our cousins. She is a respected member in family gatherings and a valuable asset for dinner conversations. I am always the silent sibling, tongue-tied and embarrassed. My sister is both my idol and my nemesis; someone I can never fully love nor truly ever hate.

My shadow-self first presented itself in an insidious whisper of doubt when I entered the same diving competition as my sister and coalesced into solid insecurity when I lost to her agility. We were seven years old when she rose above the water in a stunning swoosh of grace, while I remained trapped beneath the surface, looking up to her and striving with my failing limbs to reach the seemingly unattainable heights that she gained with poise and certainty.

"You should have won as well," my mother said to me afterward, looking over my sister's shoulders as they embraced. The last two syllables cleft our relationship like an uncrossable ravine, widening every time I remembered being measured against my sister. She has always been the unachievable standard.

Even though we are adults now, I am still her underwater reflection, a subpar mimesis left behind when she rose away into the world of social success and stability. I stayed within my murky waters, feeling undesirable and unwanted in the dark, perpetually trying to break the glassy surface of my own perception, trying in vain to enter into my sister's world.

All these thoughts and emotions churn through my mind. It is summer; she has invited me to her house in the Hamptons. We're on her yacht, and I watch her down dainty glasses of rosé champagne, a staple of her diet. I lose myself in admiration of my picturesque surroundings; the manicured estates on the shore and the polished gleam of sunlight striking the yacht remind me of my sister and her radiant, crafted smiles. I hear a panicked cry and a resounding splash before I turn around to see my sister falling into the brackish water.

I freeze. I stand in a limbo, trapped between the two most momentous decisions of my life. My sister's cry for help rings through the vacant stillness, as if condemning my betrayal. Her arms flail through empty air before she is swallowed by the waves. Seconds tick by.

Still, I hesitate, lingering on my vision of a future without her shadow.

But the future world I glimpse beyond is grim with guilt, blackened by my treachery, lifeless. My own guilty reflection stares back at me, hovering above my sinking sister.

A moment later, I throw myself into the dark waters. I dive deeper in search of my sister.

There she is, like a fading flicker in the dark, stranded by my murky indecision and drowning because of my explosive jealousy.

I latch onto my sister's limp body and struggle for the receding light at the surface. But darkness from below reaches for us like claws, taunting me with buried insecurities. My incompetence, my lack of talent, my fear for always being the second best and never good enough threaten to drag us into the abyss.

But for the first time, I fight back. The life of my sister depends on me, and it no longer matters that I am her shadow.

I picture myself stepping onto center stage and into the light. I envision love, gratitude, and acceptance for me, the shadow sister. I imagine a future where my sister and I are real sisters, and not defined by either our lightness or our darkness.

I manage to break through the surface; my life had never been as bright and clear.

On the deck of the boat, my sister opens her eyes, as if she is seeing me for the first time, without my halo of darkness.

"Don't ever leave me," I whisper.

My world is free of shadows.

The Witching Hour

Sarah Miller

The women in my family are witches.

Or so the rumors say.

They say the Montgomery girls are wicked, with sea salt and madness in our blood. We do the impossible. We worship the pagan gods. They speculate about us with fear and reverence. There are too many whispers to count, but one rumor remains the same: witch.

Nobody says it to my face, but I know what they see. Not me. They only see the mystique that surrounds me. I know they watch, looking to see if I have any magic in me, any madness. Looking to see if I'm like my sisters.

"Witch," they whisper.

Maybe they're right.

My mother can heal broken bones and delusions. My aunt can control dreams, choosing how long to leave you in a nightmare. My cousin manipulates minds, implanting thoughts that feel like your own. Her sister manipulates objects, making a pencil as deadly as any blade.

My two older sisters are twins. They are opposites. Their differences serve to complement each other. Isolde, my icy eldest sister, controls water, crafting cerulean waves and hazardous hailstorms. Isolde is clinical and calculating, always planning, and has trouble relating to anyone nonmagical.

Brigid keeps us warm with flames as vibrant as her red hair. If Isolde is the icy cold, than Brigid is the welcoming warmth. Her emotions are always on display, and she thrives on connecting with people. Brigid can relate to nonmagical people. She sees them as needing to be protected, while Isolde sees them as a nuisance.

All of the women in my family are witches, except for me.

I have no affinity for spells or creation, not a drop of witchcraft. The townspeople aren't the only ones who watch me. I know my sisters and mother are always looking for magical talent, anything that would make me like them. I offer nothing except disappointment. I am no witch.

I'm not normal either.

My power is a curse. I see the truth. I see everything people try to keep hidden: insecurities, secrets, feuds, their true selves.

I sit next to a nice girl in class. I don't see her. I see the envy that rules her; I see clothes that won't fit, friends that are prettier, missed birthdays, and bitter hugs. I forget what life was like before my curse. I was happier. I had friends. I can only neutralize my curse with deep concentration. When I'm involved with people, I'm overwhelmed.

I'm lonely. It's easier this way. It's unbearable being friends when you see people's darkest parts.

People live willfully ignorant of their friend's dark underbellies. Skeletons exist, but they can believe the best of their friends. I have no such luxury.

I'm only biding my time in this town. The supernatural is the heart of this odd hamlet. My sisters and cousins will never leave, irreparably bound to the very dirt of this place, which our own ancestors once tread. As for the citizens untouched by magic, they too are bound to this town. Most will leave for college promising never to return and upon graduation return forever.

I feel no connection. I will leave this town without looking back.

Maybe sooner, if the killings continue.

My mother would never let me leave. My aunt is already eyeing me sorrowfully, with my plane ticket written in every sad smile. She loves her sister more than anything and knows my departure would break my mother. That ticket isn't bought yet, but after every dead child, she becomes a little more anxious, browsing airline websites. My aunt will protect her sister at any cost, even if protecting my mother means betrayal.

I wish I didn't know how much this betrayal will break them.

There's special magic between sisters.

Mother may play at being unflappable, but the killings have shaken her.

Girls are taken every full moon, and a day later, their bodies are found in the sea by unsuspecting tourists.

I am surprised the villagers don't blame us, harkening back to the merciless prosecutions of old. My family is full of witches. They've always strived to help the town, healed the town's children, reaped the harvest, ended droughts, and banished evil. These killing are brutal and cruel, nothing short of wicked.

I am jolted out of my reverie by my sister and cousin.

My cousin asks, unaware of her audience, "Have you heard what Dahlia's saying?"

My sister replies, "About the killings?" She has been fascinated by the killings, searching for the perpetrator.

My cousin lowers her voice. "She's saying she might know a way to catch the killer."

Isolde starts to ask another question, when she stops, catching sight of me.

"Cassandra," she says, nodding.

I nod in return.

We're not close. She's not malicious. I don't think she quite knows what to make of me, her half-human sister.

My cousin smiles, almost asking me to join them, but follows Isolde out the door.

I hear the strains of their renewed conversation for a second just before they slip out of reach.

I'm about to start my homework when I hear a knock. I'm startled. Nobody knocks at our door. I view the peephole, not about to let a stranger in, when I see Lucy Hayes's telltale braids.

I open the door.

She bursts in without an invitation.

"Please, I need help," she says, shuddering. "It's my sister. She's missing." Her voice shakes.

Despite myself, I'm overwhelmed with pity.

Lucy will likely never see her sister again.

"I'm not sure you want my help. Maybe someone else in my family? I don't think I'm able."

Her braids sway as she furiously shakes her head.

"I don't trust the others; besides, you can read people. You can determine who took my sister."

I shake my head.

"How did you get that idea? I can't read people. I'm sorry. I don't think I can help."

I want her to leave and beg for the help of a witch. I don't want to think of the terrible power I hold, one which dooms me to isolation.

"Please, you have to help me find her. I don't want her to end up like those other girls. I don't want her to end up dead." Her body heaves with wracking sobs.

I am seized by shame.

Shame, because I know what truly motivates my reluctance to help.

Fear.

Fear of what I'll find as I search, what I'll discover about people that is best remaining secret.

And most frighteningly of all, the fear that I could've saved the girls if I'd been a little braver.

At last I ended up helping Lucy. I can't know for sure what made me do that.

Maybe it was the thought of Lucy's sweet, smiling little sister, gone. Maybe it was Lucy's fierce love for her sister, love that would destroy her, that led me to action. Or maybe it was the roiling anger that had been stirring in me for months. A fury so fervent it can only be borne of helplessness and hurt. Hurt because the town cared for its dead daughters, but accepted their deaths. When a girl was taken, the town mourned her. She was already dead to them, and there was only a paltry effort to save these girls from the inevitable. Those girls had been abandoned by their families, cared for, but their parents were resigned to their daughters' destiny.

Maybe it was because of a different sort of anger; the anger I swallowed like a bitter pill when I heard a hurried whisper in the hallway or felt a classmate's searing stare. Maybe it was the kind of hurt anger that made me clench my fists because I craved attention. The anger that blossomed from Isolde's disdain, Brigid's pity, and my mother's absolute befuddlement.

Maybe I was just tired of being weak.

"All right, I'll help in whatever way I can."

"Thank you."

Before I can respond, she embraces me.

She moves for the door, but then seems to think better of it.

She removes her necklace.

"When you find her, can you give this to her?"

"Of course," I softly promise.

Whether I find her dead or alive.

She leaves without looking back.

I know what I need to do.

My sisters always try to amplify their power, but I have no need of spells, rituals, or magical artifacts.

This power, this curse is a part of me, as integral as my heart. Utilizing it is easy. Suppressing it caused me so much strain. For so long I have been ruled by fear. Now I have no choice but to let go of my fear and see.

I think of the equilibrium my mother talks about, the feeling of completion that occurs when she heals. This is what I imagine it feels like. I am everything and nothing. I see every secret, every deed best left unsaid, and every kindness. I see hurt, shame, fear, loneliness, envy, and sorrow. I see comfort, joy, confidence, and excitement.

I see Lucy's sister.

I walk to the cliffs in a fog.

Lucy's sister is trembling, cowering before her likely death, but she still does not let loose any tears.

She sees me and moves to warn me, but I shake my head and whisper one word.

Run.

She obeys without another word, sprinting furiously down the cliff path.

I don't blame her. In fact, I understand better than most. It had taken me only moments to divine the killer's identity, but those moments had felt like trudging through molasses: long and arduous. I hadn't just seen him; I was him. I felt the sting of a father's slap, a girl's cruel, curt refusal, the sick pleasure of squeezing a slender throat with my calloused hands, and the beauty of the roiling waves.

I wait on the cliff's edge without fear. I know him, and I know there is only one way this can end.

He does not disappoint.

"I've been waiting for you." His voice is silky smooth.

"I'm sorry to have kept you waiting."

He forces me to the edge of the cliff and makes a move to push me, but I am ready.

I unsheathe my kitchen knife and stab him just as he pushes me off the cliff.

The next morning, they find me drowned in the waves, Lucy's locket wrapped around my neck.

My bones will remain rotting in the craggy soil never to leave this town.

Cassandra, I was named.

Seer.

Prophet.

Cursed.

See You in Valhalla

Mason Xavier Surratt

In a Viking village before recorded history, there lived a twelve-year-old boy named Askell. He lived on a beet farm and loved to fight anything bigger than himself. Askell's father, Colborn, was a Viking defender, shielding their village from the destruction of dragons that punished mankind's every settlement with fire.

His mom, Erling, was a Valkyrie and a veteran of the War of Radburn's Sacrifice, in which her cousin had presented herself up to Valhalla as a scorched offering for the dragons in return for mercy in a conflict the Vikings would never win.

When Askell was too young to walk, his dad had left for a battle in Lachina, a realm so cold that a warrior froze in his boots if he stopped moving between one campfire and another. Colborn had set off to join the battle against the Icelanders, cruel savages who spoke in a strange and unfamiliar tongue. Colborn never returned from the battle, and none of his comrades would speak of his death, for it made them feel ashamed to think one of their greatest warriors should fall at the hands of an army so unintelligent.

Every day, after his chores were done (hunting for rabbits and elk), Askell would go to the river, find a stick, and practice battling—pretending that he was fighting a dragon. The townsfolk looked at him like he was foolish, saying:

"Why is that boy so obnoxious?"

"Why is he always playing his stupid games?"

But Askell didn't care because his mom had always told him that only the greatest warriors are sent to Valhalla, while the cowards and weaklings are sent to Helheim to live in torment for all eternity. So he would be at that river, practicing combat almost all day, for he wanted to follow in his mother's footsteps.

Then one day while he was at the river he heard yelling and screaming in the direction of the village. When he ran back there, out of breath, he saw something he'd only read about before in books.

Death and destruction lay everywhere. Buildings lay in crumpled rubble. And as he approached the ruins, Nidhogg, a thousand-year-old dragon, burst from the cinders of the town hall. Nidhogg was known to him only as a myth but now stood before him, the symbol of devastation. Shiny scales, teeth like daggers, a face like a demon, a tail like a whip, a body like a snake, and fire as hot as Helheim.

Askell backed up and then ran, screaming, "Mother!"

As he did, Erling burst out from beneath a tent, charging at Nidhogg, and other soldiers followed her when she beckoned them.

Seeing her son, Erling threw a desperate spear forward and said, "Askell, no!" She grabbed him by the collar. "Padraig, get him underground now!"

"Yes, warlord!" said Padraig, his mother's man-at-arms, and dragged Askell, kicking and screaming, away from his mother to the Tunnels of E'trave, a long series of man-size burrows built to protect Vikings from dragon raids.

The last thing Askell saw as he was pulled into the mouth of the first cave was Nidhogg spitting flames of venom, melting his mother's soldiers, and lastly, covering his mother with an inferno.

Late that night, tears leaving his face raw, unable to sleep, he prayed to Odin that he might one day avenge his mother's death and prove he was worthy of Valhalla. He had no reason to believe either of his parents still lived, so he could only hope to see them in the next life.

Years passed. Askell grew strong, training with sword and bow under Padraig's guidance. Padraig was the closest thing to a father he had now, and the man felt beholden to Erling. He felt it was his obligation to watch over her child.

At seventeen, Askell stood a head taller than Padraig and twice as broad. He felt ready to avenge his mom. The inhabitants of his parents' village had moved to Goubellin, a fortress of obsidian, covered completely, so that neither the dragon's fire nor its poisonous venom could penetrate it.

One autumn day, while preparing a bear's hide for clothing, the horse of Havroun, Goubellin's only messenger between cities, came back without its rider, and only a note pinned to its hide, saying Nidhogg was terrorizing Talputte, a fishing village thirty miles east of the obsidian fortress.

So Goubellin sent five hundred Berserkers, men who forsake the comfort of animal skins for the speed that going bare-chested offered them in combat. In addition, the fortress sent Talputte thirty catapults, twenty war-beasts (mutants created by alchemists, consisting of six eyes and spike frills on their head and back that they used as weapons), and fifteen ballistae.

Unfortunately, all of these Berserkers and beasts were thwarted. Nidhogg was too fast and too strong. He evaded catapulted stones, slashing blades and thrashing frills. His ancient fire seemed unstoppable!

When Askell heard the news of the defeat, he asked for an audience with Sigrid, the king of the obsidian fortress. The young warrior told Sigrid that he would succeed where the Berserkers had failed.

Sigrid laughed and said, "I remember you. You're that orphan farm boy from the south. Your family does not come from combat, but crops. What are you going to use, farm boy? A hoe and spade?"

All the remaining Berserkers, drinking their mead and ale, and resentful of a lad who claimed he could achieve what they could not, laughed uproariously.

Askell said, "Fine. I don't need you to believe in me. And I don't need your permission or your help. I will go there on my own, and if I see you next only in Valhalla then so be it!"

So he set off on his quest, and he took a map to Nidhogg's lair. Though Sigrid doubted him, and believed Askell was on a suicide mission, he respected Askell's dignity and gave him a gift of obsidian armor—a shield as impenetrable as the fortress itself.

Askell felt determined but also afraid. He resented that he should be forced to go alone. "Your soul will be punished at Helheim for your cowardice," he muttered under his breath, picturing the king and the Berserkers with their mutton stuck in their beard, laughing at him.

On his map, he saw his destination would be a village called Kadri. It was a *porp* in the south. (A *porp* is a Viking word for a small village or settlement.)

Askell found an ominous cave at the edge of this *porp*. Many travelers had mistaken it for a shortcut through the mountain and had been brutally ripped apart by claws and fire.

It was locally called Helheim's Gate because anyone who entered ended up irreversibly charred or dead. Everybody feared this place. In Kadri, a young street urchin boy named Pavo told Askell he had lost his own father in that cave. The boy strangely reminded Askell of himself.

The boy was an orphan like him—no real parents. When Askell asked Pavo about his mother, the boy said she had been executed for speaking out of turn. It pained Askell to think that someone else had to suffer the fate of losing their parents, as he had.

He walked in the cave. Dead Vikings and Valkyries were everywhere. After battling humans, Nidhogg took corpses back to his lair as trophies. Askell couldn't help but shield his eyes from the slaughter.

He walked farther into the cave. More carnage. Finally, he saw Nidhogg staring at him with his crimson eyes from the dark. It made Askell feel light-headed, but he couldn't stop now. He needed to see his mom.

"I seek vengeance for my mother's death! I will cut you down, and I will see my mother in Valhalla!"

The penetrating stare from Nidhogg's eyes left Askell feeling as if Helheim was burning in his soul. The beast stood, and a massive tail swung at the Viking's feet.

Askell dodged left and swung his battle-ax at Nidhogg's tail. With an enormous thud, the tail fell to the floor. Nidhogg screamed in agony as his stub of a tail flailed around aimlessly. Then Nidhogg shot a blast of fire to Askell and he wailed. The burn hit his right arm and seared to the bone. Sprinting toward the beast, Askell felt a rush of adrenaline, for his only wish was to see his mother once again in Valhalla.

As he slit Nidhogg's right eye, the dragon screamed in pain and flailed as his empty eye socket spewed a shower of blood on the Viking. While the ancient reptile was distracted, Askell ran to heal his arm. He used some bandages that he had brought with him for his journey.

He had few of these left, for he had been attacked by a dire wolf on his way to Kadri and bitten in the ankle. The memory of that moment made his wound sting. He used the remaining bandages to wrap his roasted arm, then walked out from his hiding place and saw Nidhogg searching for him.

Askell caught Nidhogg's eye again. He charged and blasted a burst of flames that Askell had no time to evade. It hit him dead on. As Askell's skin slowly melted away, his body was filled with hatred and rage. He charged at the beast even as he burned away and unsheathed the dagger from his belt, then gripped the beast's head. He stabbed away at Nidhogg while it thrashed its body like a frightened horse. Finally, the beast fell to the ground lifeless. With his final breath, Askell got on his knees and muttered, "See you in Valhalla."

Dagger Jensen Saves the World

Maggie Watson

An evening swordfight took place as planned on a placid Sunday afternoon in suburban Indiana. Overlooking a golden sea of corn, the lone victor lingered, briskly beholding the sun as it set over his mighty empire. In his imagination, the sight before him was that of wonder and amazement expected by royalty, but the reality was much less glorious. The proud victor was just a boy, and the swordfight was with an inanimate leaf of corn. In the boy's defense, this particular leaf of corn was larger and more intimidating than most others.

Dagger Jensen, nine years old and unafraid of even the most elusive demons, was indisputably born to be a hero. He entered the world in the bathroom of a run-down diner, and his first item of clothing was a checkered tablecloth wrapped in such a way that it appeared to be a cape. And with this cape, Dagger would remain through his many years into the foreseeable future, protecting the countryside from all who dared defy him.

"Dagger, do you have pants on?" yelled a voice in the distance.

"Probably, I don't know…c'mon, Momma, I'm busy!" he whined. Everyone knows heroes cannot be expected to remember details as insignificant as pants.

"DAGGER GREGORY JENSEN," repeated his mother.

"Okay, fiiine, I'm coming," whimpered the deflated little hero.

Then, suddenly and without warning, a ferocious beast rounded the corner of the depleted dirt road. Mightier than any to grace this fair countryside, this creature was emotionless, grotesque, and unapproachable. He couldn't quite put his finger on it, but something was certainly off-putting about the being. Just as Dagger began his approach, he was interrupted by his mother once more.

"Dagger, I will take away that silly cape, young man!"

And at that, the boy was off, racing toward his house, determined to face the monster another day without risking the loss of his beloved cape.

Once within the walls of his home, he could breathe at last. The dinner table was all set, displaying three plates littered with portions comparable to the grandest feast. It was Sunday after all, and his momma never missed a chance to splurge on Sunday.

"Now you go get some pants on, Dagger. Your daddy's coming home tonight," she gushed excitedly.

"Momma, I don't think…" he started.

"Hush and get changed."

And that was that.

As much as Dagger missed his father, three years was a long time to be away. Dagger could barely remember his face. Instead, there was only a shadow of a human being too weak to support a family and too scared to defend his home. Dagger would never be too scared; fear didn't suit a hero.

As usual, Mr. Jensen did not show up that night. Even after all those years, Mrs. Jensen hadn't been able to renounce her hope. During dinner, she inquired as to Dagger's happenings that day.

"Well, that scary monster came back again. He just won't leave us alone," Dagger grumbled, bitter and perturbed.

"Oh, heaven's sake! Leave the poor old man alone and don't refer to him as a monster," she exclaimed, much to Dagger's surprise.

"We can't let him win…he's out to get us for sure!" the boy quipped.

"That poor thing has been through enough. I've never met him, but why do you think he wanders through the fields all day and night, Dagger? He most certainly has a miserable enough existence without your constant bothering and hovering and sword gestures."

After she had finished, Dagger waited a while for her to calm herself.

"Oh, Dagger, I didn't mean to raise my voice. But really, young man, what would your father think?"

Shortly after dinner, the boy crept back out to the swaying field, the moon guiding his every step. At the distant snap of a twig, he turned his head quicker than a hiccup and held his breath. After dashing down a steep hill shielded by grass twice his height, he peaked through a clearing into a riverbed just south of his house where he was sure the noise had originated.

"Ha!" he thought. "At last I have discovered the lair of my nemesis."

Indeed, he had, and one glance at the man was enough to verify his worst fears. He was rather large, skin like leather, and teeth peeking out through layers of filth. He was wearing very little clothing. The strongest waves of an ocean would not be able to rid him of the most horrid stench that followed him everywhere. Curiously, he bore a slick top hat, appearing brand-new, and creating the aura of a life lived long ago.

With a gasp, Dagger realized he had forgotten his sword. Here he was, headed into a battle, with no weapon. In his scurry to retreat, the man spotted him from the damp spot in which he lay uncomfortably.

"Come here, boy," spoke the being.

Dagger was frozen in the darkness of the grass.

"I see you standing there, and may I just remark, you have simply the best taste in fashion." With that, the man chuckled and stared fondly at the cape.

Intrigued and infuriated, Dagger slowly turned to look back and cautiously stepped out of the tall grass toward the edge of the riverbed, making eye contact with his enemy.

"Mister, I don't know what you think you're doing. But I am simply defending my home. I'd thank you not to underestimate me, especially since I'm up here while you're sittin' down in the dirt."

"My, what an intelligent young boy, and brave at that."

"Are you making fun …" began the child.

"No! No! Never!"

"Then what are you doing here?" Dagger demanded.

"I am without purpose, and I fear I have lost all hope of finding one."

Dagger sat down and looked on expectantly, as if to listen to a story.

Bearing a rare smile, the old man began his tale, altered to befit such a young knight.

"Once, there was a king and queen. They ruled over a heavenly land and desired a child to carry on their honorable legacy. Their child was a blessing, but the king was no longer receiving wealth from his kingdom. How then could he bring wealth to his family? He vowed to venture the many lands and seas in search of riches fit for a royal family, but the world greeted him with harshness and brutality."

"But he prevailed, right? Heroes always prevail," interjected the fascinated boy.

"Of course, heroes always prevail," responded the man hesitantly.

"Now it's rather late. You'd better be heading home. After all, what would your mother think?"

Dagger thought the monster had turned out to be oddly and wonderfully personable. With that, he returned to a bed where he would sleep soundly and dream of faraway kingdoms.

~~~

The sun rose the next day, and Dagger raced out to his mountain above the plains, once more awaiting the creature. But, for the first time, Dagger had no intention of harming him.
~~~

His mother had told him not to be out for long, so he only had a short time today, but he simply had to confirm that the previous night was more than just a dream.

The man appeared, with happier eyes than Dagger remembered, and Dagger ran to greet him with glee.

"Good morning, young man. Did you sleep nicely?'

"Yes, I…"

He trailed off as he noticed the man shiver from a gusting fall wind.

After removing his cape, Dagger tentatively held out the very source of his power to a complete stranger, not understanding why.

"For me?" questioned the man.

"Yes, I can save the world another time."

"Well, I'll tell you what. You just saved mine." His warm smile and kind eyes suggested sincerity, though his filth still bothered the little boy.

"Wouldn't you like to take a bath, sir?"

"No, that's mighty kind of you, though."

In that moment, Dagger's mom called him to come get bathed.

"Really, you should join me! My momma's nice too."

"No, I really ought to go."

Mrs. Jensen came running out to find out what was keeping her son when she saw the man from atop the hill. They made eye contact for an instant, then the man turned and began to walk into the grass, which swallowed him whole. Mrs. Jensen's face went pale as a bedsheet, and she ran after him, but to no avail. Like an apparition, the man had vanished into the endless rows of grass as if he was never there at all. She collapsed to her knees and began to cry.

"What's the matter, Momma. He didn't do anything!" attempted Dagger.

"How long has that man been seeing you?" she mustered.

"Well, I don't…"

"Tell me now!" she screamed.

Startled, Dagger explained the situation, which seemed only to increase her distress.

"Just tell me what's wrong, Momma," begged the teary-eyed boy.

"Foolish boy, don't you know your own father when you see him?"

And as the sun set that day, Dagger realized the man would not return. He vowed to travel the world in search of his father. He vowed to demand an explanation. Above all, he vowed to restore his family. For now, however, he would bring his mother soup and go to bed. He knew not what awaited him outside the vast prairie lands, far away from his kingdom, but he was not afraid. Dagger Jensen had sworn never to be afraid; fear did not suit a hero.

The Expired

Devanshi Bhargava

Iris Everlark. That was my name. At least, for another couple of hours. Then I'd be dead, gone from this world. All thanks to some red ink on my arm, stamped at birth, like everyone else here. The date and time at which point I would cease to exist, at the mere age of thirteen. The Society made sure of it.

This twisted idea was to ensure a perfect population of people. Apparently, it had worked. The folks in my town were serene, with no one grabbing for power and everyone accepting what life hurled at them. Of course, I didn't know *how* the Society knew when people would die. Only the Leaders knew. I had a feeling, though, that many of the intelligent, *curious* people tended to die young. People like me.

Of course, anytime I brought this matter up to my dad, he just berated me for doubting the Society. I knew I asked countless questions, and I really wasn't supposed to. That was just who I was. Tomorrow at exactly 2:47 a.m., I would be gone. Just like that.

As I stepped through the oak doors of the dwelling where my dad and I lived, the scent of a fresh cake immediately tickled my nose. My father stood there, holding the treat on a platter. I sprinted toward him as he set down the plate and engulfed me in a warm hug.

"How's my little flower?"

I crossed my arms over my chest and pouted. "Well, I'm going to die. We've been over this," I stated as my father wearily sat down.

"I've just had so much work at the Society—"

"You mean the job you aren't allowed to tell me about!" I huffed and sat down. "You can tell me! Anyone's knowledge of the secret job will die with me at—" I paused to look down at my arm. "Two forty-seven a.m."

"I wish I could, but I just can't," he responded with a rueful smile. "Besides," my father whispered softly, "I couldn't think about my little flower wilting."

I let my first tear roll down my cheek. "I'm gonna miss you, Dad," I managed to choke out.

"I'm going to miss you too, Iris…You mean more to me than you'll *ever* know."

I pulled away from his embrace and blinked the tears out of my eyes. "Quick and easy, that's how the Society claims it is, right?"

"It won't even hurt," my father replied.

I attempted a smile, but faltered. How typical of him to say that…whatever they did was right in his eyes. For all anyone knew, the Leaders in the Society could be *poisoning* the people! I caught my breath. The Society would never do that…*would* they?

I shook my head at the seemingly ridiculous thought. *Pre-death-day jitters, that was all.*

My father smiled for a moment, then disappeared into the kitchen. He came back a minute later, holding a slice of cake.

"Sweetie, the Society sent your special cake, because tomorrow, you know…"

"I'm going to die."

Setting the tray in front of me, he planted a kiss on my head. "Hopefully this will make you feel better. Just relax and try to get some sleep. Remember to wake me up when it's time."

Yeah. Time for me to die. As I ate my cake, I knew one thing. This was the last time I'd see my father again. Because where *I* was going, I wanted to be alone.

A buzzing of my smart watch at two thirty roused me from my practically nonexistent sleep. After all, how do you sleep knowing that it's the last rest you'll ever get? I promptly clicked off the alarm, overly cautious as to not awaken my dad. I didn't want him there when I…*expired.*

Now, I was headed to the woods. Grabbing my empty leather satchel, I crept downstairs and then deep into the forest. Reaching my neck of the woods, I sat down on a flat rock. Taking a deep breath, I glanced at my watch. *2:46.* One minute left. Slowly, I closed my eyes. This was it. I waited for the end to come.

And waited. And waited some more. A minute *must* have passed by now. Slowly, my eyes fluttered open, as I stared at the watch. *2:49.* Suddenly, it struck me. I had…*survived.* I stood up feeling light-headed. What do I do *now*? I couldn't go home; they'd find me. This had never happened before.

I leaned against the nearest tree, as a strange mark caught my eye. The letters *T* and *E* intertwined were carved into the bark of the weeping willow. And below it "*Libertatum.*" Liberty. This wasn't meant to be here.

I reached out, as my fingerprints lightly grazed the surface. With a quiet creak, the bark broke away, revealing a compartment within the softwood. Wonderstruck, my hand found its way inside, groping in the darkness, until it grasped some items. My adrenaline pumping, I brought them into the moonlight.

There was an old, yellow map, with a path outlined to get to the outskirts of the Society, the area still in ashes from the war that had destroyed North America a millennium ago—outside the government's control.

There was a leather notebook, which seemed to be in some code. I made a mental note to examine that later.

Finally, I carefully unfolded a newspaper article dated over fifty years ago. It seemed like a great deal had been done to hide it.

October 2075

Society's foolproof population control plan failed?

Reports suggest that there are some who have, in fact, lived through their death-date. These few kids have indeed escaped the clutches of the government. Could this be a sign that perhaps we are not as bound to these laws as we thought? Maybe we could even start a democracy, as they used to have in America. This could be the start of a new era.

No *wonder* the Society had tried to discourage this. This challenged their authority, something the Leaders couldn't stand. And it proved that I wasn't the first...*glitch.* There were others like me out there. And I needed to find them.

Suddenly, a series of shrill beeps rang out through the silent night. Alarmed, my attention was drawn to my smart watch, a required accessory for all humans. It was blowing up with messages and calls from my dad. He knew.

A light breeze rustled the strands of orange hair sticking out from my loose braid. Glancing up, I could see the tips of helicopters, as they prowled my woods. The sound of sirens drowned my ears, turning my sacred oasis into a manhunt.

Meanwhile, my watch was still buzzing and vibrating. They were getting closer…I needed to act fast.

Rushing, I dumped all of the items from the tree into the leather satchel and flung my smart watch into the shrubs. Then I *ran.* I was off the grid, with the entire nation on the search for me. I'd get to the destination on the map and figure out the Society's secrets, once and for all.

I spent the next two days following the trail, hiding in the brush when I heard the clamber of officials. Surviving off the forest, I spent my resting times unraveling bits of information that made me question my entire existence. And my *family.*

Like the fact that you don't just…*die.* The Society kills you. Their biomedical engineers have designed a drug, Nightlock, which is then placed into a cake and delivered to your doorstep. The credit for this goes to the Society's head biomedical engineer: Liam Everlark, none other than my *father.*

Also, the Society monitors you through the smart watch. That's how they know when to kill you. Their true reason for the time limits isn't to control the population and keep everyone happy. It's so that all of the outspoken people, the ones who have the potential to change the world, stay out of the way, and the Society stays in control.

Finally, what explains *me.* Some kids are immune to Nightlock. These kids' brains are more developed, thus making them intelligent and capable of overthrowing the Society. The Leaders *fear* me.

Yup. *This* is my life. I'm a glitch in the system, and my father is a murderer. Welcome to my world. *How am I still sane?*

At last, I reached the destination marked on the map. Glancing up, it seemed like a cave with a waterfall cascading in front of the entrance, hidden by the edge of the forest, the part that hadn't given way to ashes. But after deciphering the final page of the notebook, I knew *otherwise.*

If you were able to get this far, then you are one of us. Open the compartment and take the red pill, which will allow you to walk through the falls.

After flipping to the back cover, I pried open the carefully camouflaged compartment and swallowed the red pill. Closing my eyes, I walked through the falls.

After stepping through the curtain of electricity, the first thing I saw were bright blue eyes and a shock of black hair. The boy in front of me stood still.

"I'm Iris," I began, unsure of what exactly to say. I saw a slight smile grace his lips, as he held out his hand for me to shake.

"I'm Luka."

I watched as more faces emerged from the shadows.

"Who *are* you?" I asked, as the boy in front of me stared into my eyes, a fire of passion burning in his.

"We are the next generation of Leaders. The ones who have defied their lifetimes and have been hunted because of it." Luka paused, and I stared back with as much intensity as he had previously shown, daring him to go on. "We are…the *Expired.*"

Alone

Asha Patel

The beeping of the monitor is slow and steady, and I find myself growing more and more annoyed with it as time progresses. At least my heart is still beating. The silence is eerie; I would at least expect quiet murmurs from the doctors and nurses working outside of my room, but there is nothing. The blanket covering me is useless. It is doing very little to keep me warm. I wish I could ask someone to pull it up to cover my shoulders. But I can't talk, my eyes are closed, and I am stuck here.

I am stuck here smelling the pungent stench of bleach. I am stuck here judging the time of day from the noises outside of my room. Sometimes I hear cries, mostly of pain and agony. I am surrounded by mourning families, but my room remains empty. But at least that annoying monitor beeps on. At least I am still breathing.

Last week, I left my apartment at seven, just like normal. I unlocked my bike from the rack outside my apartment building and mounted it with my satchel around my shoulder. When I bike, the wind ruffles my hair, and I can look around and see all the wonders of the city. There are cars packed at every stoplight, honking and inching forward impatiently, but I love to watch them as I ride by. Sometimes I take a detour so I can pass the ferry boats on the Hudson; they glide along like swans moving slowly through the water.

Every morning I bike to a coffee shop about a mile away from my apartment, where I can peacefully work. The interior of the coffee shop always feels warm, even when the frostiness of winter raps on the windows. There is constant noise, and the tapping of working fingers on computer keys is accompanied by the coffee machines in a wondrous symphony of sound. The warmth of a cup of coffee in my hands takes me back to my childhood, when I would sit in front of the windows so the morning sun could hit my face and I could smell the beautiful aroma of my mother's freshly ground coffee beans.

On Monday of last week, I biked there as usual, with my laptop in my satchel so I could do work while I was at the shop. I decided to take the long way, because in the summer, the ferry boats are packed with tourists snapping pictures and admiring the skyline. I stopped to look at one that had just docked, and I could almost see the individual faces of the people onboard. I admit, I should've been paying attention, but clearly the person driving the car was captivated as well, maybe by a text message. He hit me head on, and my satchel was flung off my shoulder as I plummeted to the ground. That's about all I can remember.

I was immediately driven in an ambulance to the nearest hospital and whisked into an operating room. Since then, I have found myself a prisoner to my own mind. I have decided in the week I have been lying here that I hate this place. I hate that I can't talk, and I hate how it smells, and I hate that I can't see the television, and I hate that they don't even switch it on for me.

Probably because the doctors and nurses don't understand that I am just as present as the rest of them. When there are slow days, I try to listen as much as possible to the conversations happening outside. Sometimes the nurses that come to check on me and fix the machines will gossip about other staff members, and I wish I could tell them that I enjoy their company. I crave the day that I can walk out of here.

I was dreaming of the city for many hours before I began to hear familiar voices outside of my room. It must be that time. My parents have been unreachable for the past week, as they have been on a cruise to the Bahamas. The hospital has been attempting to contact them from the moment I arrived here, and they were promptly notified the moment they came home. They drove to the hospital from Newark, hopefully to figure out a plan of action with my doctors. But when I hear the sound of my mother's voice, it is coated in sadness. I can hear whispers of words, especially "organ damage" and "long term."

When my parents entered my room, my mom was immediately at my side. I can feel my mother's forehead on my shoulder. She is shaking with silent tears. The droplets of water run their course along my arm, and I can hear small taps as they hit the bedsheets. My father is sitting next to the bed, and I can feel him shaking as he holds my limp hand.

I think I am dying. When I was a kid, I was never alone. Even when I was a baby, I would cry when anyone would leave me by myself. Most nights, my parents were forced to cradle me in their arms until I was asleep. I was the kind of kid who flourished when I was surrounded by people. As a toddler, I would light up when company would come over, moving from person to person and babbling for hours. I've always been an extrovert, and my parents have adapted accordingly. That is why I expected to spend the last moments of my life surrounded by all of my friends and family members. I didn't anticipate that I would be here, with only my parents by my side. They are saying their goodbyes. I want to tell them that I love them, and I want to yell at the doctors to fix me. I need them to fix me because I have a whole life ahead of me. I need them to fix me so that I can go back to the coffee shop and go back to riding my bike through the streets.

The monitor slows its tempo for the first time since I arrived here. I didn't expect this. I don't feel like I'm falling, and I know it's not my time. I am trapped in my mind, watching my life come to a close. A steady tone is emitted from the monitor, and I am alone. Completely and utterly alone.

Wisps of Hope

Jacqueline Hunter

"Shhh!" Mam whispers, scolding me for my childishness.

I lower my head, ashamed, and notice crimson blood gushing from my swollen toe. *Dang,* I think, slipping off my too small shoe to examine the damage, letting me out of my misery. It wasn't my fault it was too dark to see. My eyes catch a still form of my sister, Christie. Her most prominent feature was her vast moonlike eyes. She turns away, her tattered ivory nightgown flowing down behind her. I grit my teeth and start to hobble.

The moon peeks out of the mythical clouds. Rats skitter around my feet, and shadows appear to be lurking in every alley. Every sound makes my stomach knot up. I glance back to our shack, its exterior exactly like the others'. I hope I will never see it again.

Suddenly a memory flashes through my mind. I can remember the fateful day as clear as water. You would have never imagined ripples creasing that water.

I sat in a discarded easy chair outside our house enjoying the waft of breeze stroking my toes. I kneeled to put on my work shoes for I knew Mam would be back soon and I would need to go and be of assistance to Master William. My ears caught the sound of the unmistakable sharp footsteps walking up the road. I leaped up, and Mam stiffly marched up to me and told me to "getta move on." I ran up to Master William's "castle" and hurried in and trotted up to the master's room…

Me and Mam walked home, and I told her about the lashing Master had given me. She just shook her head and cursed him. As we approached the street, I saw a whole crowd gathered up right in front of our shack! Mam ambled up to the house as fast as she could, trying to keep off her bad leg, worried that my sister was hurt. The crowd parted as Mam came up. Some people bowed their heads and others just watched us, their beady eyes scorching through my scalp. I put my hand on Mam's shoulder.

"This ain't gonna be a pleasurable surprise," I told her in a hushed tone. I was right.

My heart was jerked out of my mouth as I glimpsed the bloodcurdling sight. My old man was slumped on our stoop, his sharp, rigid eyes staring at me unseeingly, his tattered hand-me-down old beige shirt shredded open. His back was gashed open, probably with a whip I realized. Mam made a throttling sound as she lurched on her side. I choked back my tears and horror and caught her and led her inside, knowing I would never get that gruesome image out of my mind.

Once Mam had calmed down (her wails turned into whimpers and day turned into night), we had a conference as to what we had to do. In the end, it was decided we were going up south to her kin's house. That leads me back to the present day.

Mam had heard of something called the Underground Railroad, and her jaw was set firm, and when Mam makes up her mind, the decision's final.

~~~

The first chipped rays of dawn, like the cracks appearing on porcelain, greets us as we step out of our slum area. As we walk, Mam stops and hoists Christie onto her stooping shoulders and shuffles down the road, a lone figure on the morning horizon. I am left dumbstruck as she walks on. All I could do is oblige, and I trot like a dog behind them.

Christie whimpers, "We have been walkin' for hours, Mam."

Mam grumbles, "Now, Christie."

I berate gently, although I am secretly relieved. My legs are killing me.

"I reckon it's time to stop," Mam finally says.
~~~

I sigh in relief. We all plant our butts on the cool dirt. I see a boy selling newspapers so I get up and bring one back for Mam. She examines it, and without a warning, she gasps. “Look at this.” She spits.

I peer over her shoulders with curiosity. The Confederate is winning victories left, right, and center, and the Gettysburg battle is yet to happen. “Beware!” the text shrieks up at me. A sudden realization seems to come over me, kinda like the eureka moment. We are in Gettysburg right now! My eyes meet Mam’s, and we both know what we need to do. The Union needs supporting, and it is time to do the right thing. Maybe, there is hope for people like us after all! A thread of hope seems to unravel in my chest.

Hope was what kept you going, without hope…you would never survive…

I notice a throng of people who look like us in uniforms. I know they must be in the Union!

I motion for everyone to follow me as we creep up to the people. “Pardon us, where are ya goin’ if I may ask?”

The men turn at the sound of my voice.

“Now who said that?” says an old-looking one, peering at me.

I clear my throat and answer, “Me, sir, with all due respect, sir.”

“Ya don’t find many youngins talkin’ with respect these days,” he croaks.

My chest swells…

Mam clears her throat. “Sir, we were wondering if we could help in the battle for Gettysburg,” she says softly.

“Well, I’ll be. Of course ya can!”

It seems like a ray of hope cuts through the dark times we are facing.

“Now how old are ya?” he wheezes.

“Fourteen years old, sir,” I say, my throat dry.

“That means you can help us with the fighting, and your missus and the cute little gal can help the women cook.”

Mam and Christie are ushered away.

"Now ya follow me here, sonny," a younger guy named William says, leading me away.

We walk in silence until curiosity gets the better of me, and I ask about all the people who have pale skin.

"Not all of 'em are bad, sonny," he says. "Sure, the Confederates ain't good, but trust me, our world is filled with blessed souls too. Everyone has light and darkness in them. Ya just gotta fight to have more light in ya."

He speaks with a wistful look of pride. Suddenly, a gunshot rings out followed by a shriek from ahead. We start to sprint. A big blob of gray and blue seems to be swallowing up the ground and coming closer and closer. I point this out to William, and his eyes widen with fear.

Meanwhile the Union soldiers seem to be trampling each other to get to the weaponry room. William shoves a rifle and a uniform into my hands and grabs a rifle for himself. He leads me toward a clay wall, saying no matter what I ain't gonna move. I nod. With that, he jogs away to his team who are stalking the "blob."

I put on the loose uniform. William runs back five minutes later and motions to me wordlessly to follow him. I do. Apprehension and worry are building up inside my gut. I am actually gonna fight, kill people… Can I really do that? Can I sever futures like that? Watch the light flee a victim's unseeing eyes? I know these people are trying to chain my future and many innocent black people's lives to serve the whites "who are apparently superior to us," but they are only human…

I tighten my grip on the rifle, sweat sliding over my fingers. I join the rest of the soldiers, and the mood is tense. Today could end horribly, and a massacre might occur, but hopefully it won't impact the union.

I hear a brutal cry of outrage, and I'm pushed forward by the crowd. I hear the impact of metal thwacking flesh and the ping of guns. The sun shines over me, bathing my body in light, and with the wind whistling, I feel hope. I breathe in fresh air, and adrenaline courses through me, and all my doubts are gone, and at that moment, I know I'm where I'm supposed to be.

Lily Learns Love

Hilary Barkey

Once upon a time, there was a girl named Lily. She was six years old, and her two moms took very good care of her. She had a wonderful home life, and she always had all the toys she wanted. The only problem was that none of the other kids would play with her. Lily was very lonely, so she would eavesdrop on them constantly, and she heard a lot of puzzling things. One such thing uttered was, "I can't believe that her moms love each other. Everybody should have a dad!"

She cried a lot because kids were always saying mean things like that, even though she didn't completely understand what they were saying. She was scared of them, though, because she was a lot smaller than them. She never confronted them. "One day," she thought, "I will let those kids know that I am not a bad person and that they should play with me!" However, she never found the strength to stand up to them. She would come home every day from school in tears and ask her moms why nobody liked her. "Is it because I'm adopted?" she would ask.

They assured Lily that it didn't have to do with her. Late at night, when her moms thought that Lily was asleep, she would press her ear against her wall and listen to them. She loved her moms with all her heart, and she especially loved listening to them sing late at night together and chat peacefully. This particular night, though, she didn't hear any of that. Her moms sounded really angry, saying that they should have found a set of parents that could give Lily a better life than they could, especially considering Elizabeth's health. "Elizabeth, you shouldn't be running around this much! Your condition is fragile," said her younger mom, Daisy.

Lily started crying because she didn't understand why her moms didn't think that they should be her parents. She went into the room next door with a fiery attitude to confront them. "Why do you want to give me away?" asked a heartbroken Lily.

"Why would you ever say a thing like that? We love you!" her older mom, Elizabeth, said.

"Because you said that you shouldn't have adopt—" Lily started bawling.

"Oh no, Lily, we didn't mean that we don't love you. Did we, Elizabeth?" said Daisy.

"No, of course we didn't mean that," agreed Elizabeth. "We love you so much, more than anything in the world. You are just so awesome that you deserve the best parents, and we want to make sure you have that. Why don't you go back to sleep now, Lily? You have a big day tomorrow at school."

"Okay, fine. But we never got ice cream today after school. Promise me I can have a little taste of ice cream with breakfast?" said Lily.

"Sure, honey. We love you so much!" Elizabeth said.

Lily went back to sleep, but she didn't forget her moms' angry words. The next day, she had her ice cream with breakfast, as promised. When she went to school, all of the kids were mean to her again. They wouldn't let her play any games with them, and they called her mean names like "weirdo" and "outsider." She let them torment her because she felt like she didn't belong there.

Her moms continued the heated discussions for many days, and Lily started to lose her spark. She felt like she didn't have a real home because she was adopted and her parents didn't seem to want her. She felt like she should just disappear and the world would be better off without her.

After a particularly good day of school when the bullies weren't as mean, Lily came home with her grades and showed them to her moms. “Look, I am so smart!” she proudly said to them, hoping to distract them from their arguing.

“Great job, honey,” they both said. “Why don’t we celebrate with a little ice-cream party, just the three of us?”

“Sure!”

“Great. Let’s go!”

They walked out, moms holding Lily’s hands. As Lily’s parents were telling her how proud they were of her report card, Elizabeth suddenly fell to the ground. Lily and Daisy tried to wake her up, to no avail. They called 911, and the ambulance arrived a tense ninety seconds later. Lily and Daisy rode in the ambulance, and Lily got really scared.

“Will Mommy be okay?” Lily asked.

Daisy didn’t answer but hugged Lily tight.

When they finally got to the hospital, the doctors explained that Elizabeth’s cancer had spread throughout her body. They said that she had six months to live.

Lily couldn’t believe it. “Why?” she asked.

Nobody had an answer.

For the next six months, Lily watched as Elizabeth got sicker in the hospital. Her hair fell out, and she couldn’t eat anything. Lily watched as her beautiful, strong mom got reduced to someone who could barely walk and talk. Most of the time, Lily didn’t even want to go to the hospital to see her because there was no Elizabeth left in that person. That was someone else, she insisted. That couldn’t be her mother!

During that time, though, Elizabeth was always there for Lily, cheering her on whenever she could. Whenever Lily came into Elizabeth’s room, number 211, Lily was always the priority. How she was doing at school, what she was eating at home. In a month, Elizabeth passed away, and Lily and Daisy were devastated.

Lily thought of how courageous Elizabeth had been and decided to be courageous herself. “I can do anything if I am strong like Mommy!” she said to herself.

When she went back to school, she was a little anxious.

She was thinking about confronting the bullies, but they were really big and mean. They tormented her at school during recess, calling her the usual names. She summoned all of her strength and told them to back off.

Nobody had ever stood up to them, and they were surprised. Lily used her words and told them that they were really hurting her feelings and they shouldn't act that way. They fired back some nasty comments, but she let them bounce right off her. Lily stood her ground and wouldn't let them make her sad.

None of the bullies ever dared to be mean to her again. She found her inner fire and emerged victorious.

After she finally stood up to the bullies, she asked Daisy why those kids had always been so mean to her.

"I really want to know now, Mommy. Please?" "Okay, I guess you are ready to hear this now. It was because of your mommies. Those people wanted our family to be separated because they thought that two women shouldn't love each other. That it was wrong for us to be a family."

"Why would they ever think that?"

"I don't know, Lily. All I know is that I loved Elizabeth more than anyone else in the world besides you, no matter what those kids said. I love you too, Lily."

"I love you, Mommy."

Red

Anuksha Ram Madhan

My name is Raissa Nirere.
I am forty-two years old.
I am the mother to three children.
Death shall never touch them.
For she told me no more would be taken from me.

There are people in this world who claim Death to be the beginning of a new journey. They call Death their salvation.

Those are the people who have never brushed past Death. Who've never shivered from her cold breath upon their necks, her sharp gaze piercing their own. Those are the people who have never felt primal terror as they watched her walk down a massacre, her cloak flying behind her despite the lack of wind, tainted with the color of innocent blood. And yet, they claim she is an eternal peace.

Was she not the one who turned friend upon friend and family upon family every moment since humanity took a step on the planet? Was she not the one who found joy in the loss of life in my country?

Admittedly, terror played a part in her arrival to my nation. Terror bred hatred, and hatred bred evil, and evil brought Death to our lands. And then, she proceeded with her ravaging. She fed off fear and evil. She prospered in the wake of misery.

That wasn't salvation. That was slaughter.

Death is without mercy, and even the evil fear Death.

~~~
~~~

This story began on a spring day during April of 1994 when I, Raissa Nirere, lost everything I knew.

Born to a prestigious Rwandan couple in the country's capital of Kigali, I grew up in the large city as the middle child of five siblings. I reckon I was like any other child of the upper middle class. I grew up with clean clothes on my back each night and more than enough food on my plate during each meal. I had friends I could confide in and enemies who I detested, as any teenager did. I attended a decent school, and I grew up well educated. I had changing ambitions; one day I wanted to be a teacher, the next I wanted to travel space as an astronaut. But I had never seen myself as anything but normal, and it never occurred to me to think otherwise. I suppose I considered myself utterly invulnerable to the ever-changing schemes of fate. Alas, I was not as untouchable as I had assumed.

To this day, I do not wish to know the full details of the airplane bombing that set off the chain of events that ripped life as I knew it from my hands. All I know is what I heard on the small radio in our living room as our family sat around it. I knew Rwanda had two ethnic groups, the majority Hutu and the minority Tutsi. The Hutus and the Tutsis had been at odds for centuries, and the Hutus had power again after the Tutsis had held it for centuries. I was a Tutsi, and I knew the Hutus were thirsty for retribution. And as the sun set on that sunny April day, I remember only what the radio told us: the Hutu presidents of Rwanda and the neighboring Burundi had been shot down. The Hutus claimed it was the Tutsi cockroaches. And the Hutus wanted the cockroaches dead. And everything from then onward would shape the rest of my life.

With the country falling apart within the span of hours, terror arose. And with terror arrived Death, prepared for carnage. And she had wasted no time in starting.

Thus, as the sun set on that April day in 1994, the Tutsi population of Rwanda were served dinner, but they were served not their staple cassava, but terror, served on a cold platter prepared by Death herself.

~~~

In the following days, my family packed a small satchel for each person, and we left our home in Kigali to escape with our lives. We left for the outskirts of the town and raced toward the Rwandan border.

In the first few weeks following our departure, all I could see was red. I saw scarlet in my papa's grief as he heard news of his missing brother. I saw crimson in the blood of the Tutsis who were massacred by their own nation. I saw ruby in the rage of the Hutus who hunted for their next victims. And I never wanted to see red again. I wished for a life where I could be color-blind.

Alas, as the saying went, wishes never come true.

~~~

Before I knew it, the one fateful day that would turn my life around had arrived. I didn't know it then, but it was about four weeks before the widely recognized "end" of the horrific events in Rwanda. *If only we'd lasted that long.* Regardless that my family was sleeping on a mud floor near cow dung, regardless that my younger brother Étienne was so sick he was blind, and regardless that we were being hunted like savage beasts, that morning I woke up never once contemplating the horrors that could occur that day. *Oh the irony.*

It started as it always had for the past few months: we would each eat whatever scraps we could for that day. *We ate bread that morning.* And then Papa would leave along with Benite and Jacques, my two older siblings, to try to gather resources for us to leave Rwanda. Maman would take care of Étienne, who'd been sick for months then, and I would act as their lookout. Later on in the day, Papa, Benite, and Jacques would return, more often than not empty-handed. That evening, however, that was not the case.

On that fateful evening, two returned in the place of three, and as they opened the door, Papa and Benite were covered in red. The crimson of our family's Tutsi blood. I don't remember if Benite was ever hurt, but Papa's red came from the gaping wound on his neck, which cut through his skin in a precise and deliberate manner. Papa and Benite never told us what happened that day. To this day, upon mention of that fateful day, I wonder what had passed that day that led to the still silence Benite adopted until her final moments. And in the deepest, darkest pits of my soul, I know that I would never want to know what lead to the first loss of our family: Jacques, the same lively boy who had taught me how to ride a bicycle and the boy full of soul who had comforted me when I had gotten in trouble after getting into a fistfight.

As the day went by and the darkness set upon the small barn, for the first time, I heard rusted copper in the sobs of grief my mother and Benite choked out as they lost Papa to Death's cold grip. Étienne was too sick to understand what was happening and I was simply numb. I could only remember Papa's bizarre laughter and his crinkling eyes and the simple fact that I would never again witness the phenomenon that was Papa's happiness.

Soon afterward, when Benite never returned from her run for rations, I knew that the Nirere luck had run out. We had managed to evade the brutal massacres for months, but when little Étienne, who had just regained his mental clarity, screamed in heartache for his Benite and his Jacques and his Papa, I knew we had lost.

And the rest of the story is quite simple, similar to she who carved it out. Within days, we had run out of rations, and we had no choice but to starve to death or be massacred. Maman wanted to die on her own terms, and she told me as much as she barricaded the last of the Nirere bloodline in the small barn. And when a knock came to the door, Maman handed me a large metal rod and told me to run.

I didn't question her command.

Étienne was still incapable of movement, but with the little strength I had, I dragged him with me as I slammed out a panel in the back of the barn. I couldn't help but try to stay, watch, and help Maman, but she had opened the door, and before I had the chance to look back, all I heard was a sickeningly wet smack. I knew that if I looked, she would be red.

I never found out who killed her, for Étienne and I had managed to make our getaway, not without much difficulty, and ended up at the border, from which we found ourselves in a decent town. A lady whose name was Benite led us to the safe camps.

Étienne lost his leg when they amputated it, and I had lost so much weight that I was nothing but a flap of skin on bones.

We recovered, as we'd hoped, but neither Étienne nor I have stepped foot back in the outskirts of Kigali since we lost everything. When I turned twenty-one without my family, I made a deal with the being who shaped my story the most: Death. I asked that she would never touch any children I had for she had taken so much from me. And this is where my story stays today:

My name is Raissa Nirere.
I am forty-two years old.
I am the mother to three children.
Death shall never touch them.
For she told me no more would be taken from me.

A Duel

Anna Westwig

The full heat of the Caribbean sun beat down on his shoulders, and his skin glistened with sweat he couldn't afford to lose. Sunburns clung to his umber skin in angry dark red splotches like burrs. The entire crew had been toiling beneath the sun's oppressive rays for weeks without a brush of wind to cool them. The crew had been getting antsy, of course. They were thirsty for water and blood. Today, Abshir would provide them with both.

He surveyed the ocean, his dark eyes searching the horizon with intensity. If there was land, they would not have to do this. No one would have to die. But each crew member had scanned the ocean with unusual diligence, and each one had found nothing but palaces of glittering silver sunlight, mirages dancing on the waves.

He drummed his fingers on the wooden grip of the pistol and adjusted his stance against the deck. The other men crowded around the edges of the deck, some staring longingly at the ocean as though it would somehow become safe to drink. His resolve tightened. Mako, the captain, had been lounging in his cabin, swigging from the water stores, safe in the shade, while his men shriveled like sun-dried plants.

He pulled out his pistol examining the barrel scrupulously. He took a rag hanging from his belt and polished it clean. It was a pointless ritual, but it gave him some comfort.

Abshir met his friend Ula's gaze, and he nodded. Ula responded in kind. It was a slight motion, but Abshir saw how the sharp lines of his face cut through the air.

He might never see that face again. His breath caught in his chest, but Abshir hid it and pushed down the fear. It fluttered inside his rib cage like a butterfly with razor blades for wings.

He should not be afraid. Every single member of this ship knew he was the best shot in this whole godforsaken ocean. Still, Abshir had never felt this kind of fear before. Without the frenzy of the battle to drown out this creature curling inside of him, he had forgotten how to kill. He would remember. He had to if he wanted to live and if he wanted water.

The captain emerged from his cabin wiping down the muzzle of his pistol nonchalantly. His skin was pockmarked with scars. Even he had not been unable to escape the dangers of the sea. The Atlantic did not differentiate between captains and servants; it starved them alike.

"Do you really want to go through with this?" Ula hissed at him.

Abshir stared at the cocky expression on the captain's face and then down to Ula's face scrunched up in worry.

"Yeah"—he flexed his index finger on the trigger—"I do." He choked the words out as he looked down on Ula, who stood a good inch shorter than him. Ula shook his head and stepped away to join the cluster of men on the sides of the ship. "But, Ula." He called after him, "If I do die, you get my rations."

"Then hurry up already," Ula joked.

"Sorry, I might have to disappoint you."

"Pity." Ula's face twisted into a forced grin.

"If we're done with the goodbyes." Mako sneered. "Let's get on with the duel."

"Of course," Abshir drawled, filling his throat with ennui. Anxiousness was a sign of weakness, so he would be the opposite of anxious. He should not be afraid. He knew Mako and he was a terrible shot. Abshir, however, could hit a target at a hundred paces. This would be child's play.

Abshir's mouth was suddenly dry, and he licked his lips, the pink tip of his tongue so parched it stuck to the skin. He took five paces back, his feet familiar with the warped wood. The deck had been splashed with saltwater for five years now. And its helm had been guided by Mako for just as long. Did Abshir have the right to take the ship's helmsman away from it? He couldn't answer that question.

After taking a shallow breath, he raised his pistol, the silver barrel gleaming in the sunlight. The light obstructed Abshir's view, and he cursed the captain for giving him the side facing the sun. It wouldn't matter.

Abshir was a fine marksman, and at this distance, he would hit Mako without question.

One of the crew stepped forward and counted them off, his voice scratchy. Sweat trickled down Abshir's forehead.

"Three…two…" Abshir narrowed his eyes and tightened his grip on the pistol. "One…"

His finger twitched on the trigger, and the man yelled go. He let the bullet fly faster than he could think.

The shot shattered the stagnant air as if it were made of glass. He heard Mako scream before the scent of gunpowder hit his nose. Blood poured out of a bullet hole in Mako's stomach, staining the deck red.

People often described duels as happening in slow motion: the bullets humming through the air as though it were molasses. It happened in a heartbeat. One second the bullet was in its chamber and his finger pulsed along to the rhythm of his heart, and then Mako was sprawled across the deck of his ship, bleeding out.

Abshir cringed. He had hit Mako in the stomach; his death would not be easy. He could hear the thrum of Mako's heart pumping out blood onto the deck, seeping into the wood. He had to kill him, if only to end his suffering. He took careful aim and shot at Mako's head. It pierced through his temple, and Mako slumped to the deck, blood still pouring out of him.

"Abshir wins," the announcer crowed. As if anyone needed that conformation. Their loyalties were easily turned to those who fed them. There was not much sadness in their eyes as they hoisted Mako onto their backs and tossed him into the glassy sea.

Abshir watched as the ocean grasped at the captain's body. He didn't sink but instead bobbed steadily away from the ship's hull. He couldn't avert his eyes as he watched swirls of pink mix with the ocean. He knew that Mako would become food for birds and fish alike. It was no burial for a ship captain. It was no burial at all.

He stumbled away from his position and clung to the railing of the deck. All eyes followed his path, and he remembered why he had done this in the first place. Water. They would have water. He ordered his trembling legs to carry him to the captain's cabin and retrieved jugs of water. He handed them out to the men, and they grabbed them with dry hands and shining eyes. They drank, and he could've sworn the stale liquid was the finest wine known to man.

Around an hour later, after Mako's body had been taken out of sight, a wind stirred the sails and a single droplet of rain bounced off Abshir's sweaty skin. It was as though Mako's death had been a sacrifice. Death was never justified, but the life seeping back into the crew would comfort Abshir in his troubled nights to come.

Robbed with Nickels

Sherry Sun

She looked at them with eyes full of love, but yet she could not bring herself to give them what she wanted to. She always dreamed of her perfect life—a burning fireplace and a house filled with the sweet aroma of cooking. What she has now was nothing like what she had pictured.

No one knew how it happened. No one could explain the market, or the crash, or the downward spiral that caused every man to wander in the streets.

She looked out to the sign that she knew she would regret putting out, but she had no choice.

"Four Children for Sale. Inquire Within."

She put her face in her hands, devastated. She allowed her mind to wander over the faces of her precious darlings, what she would tell them when the time came, and how she would ever be able to let go.

She started with Edward, the tallest and the oldest of them all. She remembered the joy she felt at the sight of his little face and his little hands balled into fists. She knew he was a little brave warrior from that very moment. Edward always knew how to help. She smiled at the memory of how he had fearlessly picked up a spider a few years back when his sisters had screamed and cried at the sight of the creature. He had placed it outside the door then turned back to comfort his sisters.

Her mind then went to Maria and her sparkling deep blue eyes. She had a melodious laugh that could warm anyone's heart and a beautiful singing voice that would always put little Will to sleep. If not for the market's crash, she would have sent her to the local music conservatory years ago.

Then came Helen. Helen had the greatest imagination of them all. Every day, she would tell enchanting tales of a kingdom where all dreams would come true. She gathered the wonders of her brothers and sisters then wove them into a perfect story where everything was as good as it could be. And last, there was Will. Will had barely learned to talk, but laughed with his siblings and danced around with them.

Her babies, ones she dedicated all her love to. She couldn't bear to—

"Mama," a little girl called, "there is a lady at the door."

She turned to see Maria, holding the hand of her little sister and looking nervously out the window.

"Sweetie, why don't you go see what your brothers are up to? I will go talk to the nice lady. Hurry now." She gave her the best smile one could forge and then exhaled before swinging open the door.

The lady looked about the same age as her, with an apron tied around her skinny waist, looking curiously over her shoulders.

"The sign outside," the woman said then stared at her. "Where are the children?"

She swallowed nervously then motioned for the woman to come in. After closing the door, she mumbled, "Right this way." The woman followed her as she made her way to the living room.

Edward looked up at the entry to the stranger and then nudged his siblings to drop their hands.

The woman broke into a grin. She made her way to the four children, walking around them and examining each of their features. After several moments of pacing back and forth, she pointed at Helen and then asked, "How much for this one?"

"Fifty nickels," she responded.

"Fifty! Are you out of your mind? I swear no one will have that much to offer. I say thirty," the woman argued.

She looked at little Helen with her eyes shining, finding it more and more difficult to control what she feared to come. She spat out, "Thirty-five, then she is yours."

The woman took out a little bag and counted the coins, placing them on the counter before turning to look at Helen. "Come on now. Get your things and we will be on our way."

Helen looked startled. "Mama, where am I going?"

She felt a little tug in her heart, but said, "Go get your little blanket and doll, sweetie. Mama will be at the door waiting for you."

The little girl scrambled to the next room, leaving her siblings behind. She walked toward the front door with her little blanket and patched doll, looking into her mother's eyes in search for an answer.

She kneeled down to brush Helen's hair from her face and kiss her cheeks one last time. "The nice lady is going to take you to a land of wonders, my love. You will have a lot of fun with her." She felt another tug in her heart, this time stronger. The woman paced impatiently as she pulled Helen in for a hug. "We will miss you while you're gone. Be good, okay?"

Little Helen nodded and followed the woman out the door. She watched as they disappeared onto the streets, then she felt a little crack in her heart.

She pulled the curtains shut and made her way to the living room. After counting up the coins she had received, she placed them in a barely filled jar as a small tear rolled down her cheeks.

"Mama, where did Helen go?" Maria walked up to the counter with her eyes full of confusion and concern.

She wiped the tear away before responding. "Helen left to go to a land of wonders, sweetie. We might not see her again until a very long time."

Just then, pounding came on their door. It was followed by a few disapproving comments. "Stay here with Edward and look after Will," she told the girl before dragging her feet to the door. She slowly turned the doorknob and came face-to-face with an old couple and a man, who looked a little weary. She looked at them, then asked, "Are you guys here for the sign?"

"Of course we are! Why else would anyone be here at this time of the day in this pessimistic place? These old hags followed me when I told them there were some children being sold. Ain't I right? Heh?" The man turned to stare at the old couple, who slowly nodded to confirm his statement.

She stared at these people, wondering what they might want from her children.

"Well, where are your kids?" the man questioned.

"Um, follow me please," she replied without knowing what she had just done.

The three strangers stepped into the living room and stopped. Suddenly, it seemed as if the air had been filled with the smell of alcohol and cigars. The drunk man approached Maria and then looked at her up and down. "I will take this one. Name your price, lady." He turned to look at the mother.

Maria's eyes lit up with fear as her mother responded, "Seventy nickels, or nothing." She had hoped the man would back away, but coldness drained through her as the man pulled out a bag full of coins to lay out seventy nickels right before her eyes.

"It's a deal." He grinned before turning to grab Maria by the arm and pull her out the door.

"Mama! Mama, I don't want to go with him! Please, mama, please don't let me go! I don't wan—" Maria's voice trailed off as the man slammed the door after his exit.

She felt another crack in her heart, and it came with a wave of pain. She slowly turned toward the old couple that remained. Her eyes looked lifeless as she whispered, "I am done selling for today."

"You can't do that! We want the boy! The tall one!" the old woman frantically yelled before pulling Edward to his feet.

"Let me go!" Edward pulled free before scrambling to protect little Will from the strangers.

"Oh, you will learn to talk! How much for this one? We can give you a hundred!" the old man demanded.

"I am not selling anymore," she whispered again, looking up to see Edward, struggling to fight against the old man's grip.

"Well, miss, we want the boy, and your sign tells us you are selling. We are taking him! Here are a hundred nickels. You cannot complain." The old man threw the bag of coins onto the counter and then hurried his wife to take the boy out.

"Let go of me! Can't you see my mother needs me? My brother needs me! Let go!" Edward helplessly fought as the couple pushed him out the door.

She rose to her feet. Carrying the crying Will, she rushed out the door, getting one last look at her little warrior being dragged into a carriage.

Her heart shattered into thousands of pieces.

She mourned at the unchangeable reality before turning to destroy the sign that she had made. She held Will tight and rushed back into her house, slamming the door and crumbling onto the floor.

Her children, her treasures, robbed with the nickels on her counter.

The New Kid

Sequoia Ayers

"How about her?"

"Six. She just *looks* scary to me. When she looked over this way, her eyes pierced into my innermost thoughts! And her bag is bulging on all sides, and she's super tall, too tall, and I just don't like the look of her. I'm glad I don't have to see her again!"

"Oh, you are just overreacting. She's only a three. She looks exhausted, which explains the baggy outfit. The bag is full of groceries—that you can just tell from observations. Since we are sitting at a bench outside of Trader Joe's helps." A chuckle escaped her lips as she spoke.

The sound of a car door slamming and screeching breaks were heard before the girl continued to speak. "She was in a rush to get to who knows where and was frantically looking for her car. That was why she looked over here. I don't know why you felt pierced to your 'innermost thoughts' as you put it. She is definitely not any kind of threat."

"But why is she a three?"

"I'll explain. All humans over the age of twenty-one always begin a level two, for multiple reasons. Mainly because they have the mental capacity to understand what potential ways of harm there are. However, she acquired another level because of her tendency of drunk driving and the threat she poses to her family due to her strict parenting."

"Ooohhh…I don't get it."

Another chuckle. This time she allowed her lips to curve slightly upward as well. "How am I ever supposed to teach you these things if you never understand what I am talking about?"

"Well, I am only eight."

"Fine, enough training for today. Let's go get some ice cream."

The girl walked off at a steady pace, knowing full well that her baby brother would be trailing right behind trying to catch his sister's fingers that moved so fast. It was always a fun race, and a great way to get the boy to move places at a fast rate.

~~~

On the outside, Meg Taylor appears to be just a regular seventeen-year-old kid, but an average high school student wouldn't even be able to comprehend the ability that she has. That is the exact reason she never speaks of her "gifts," as she likes to call them. Only her parents and baby brother know of her ability; even then, it's her mother who is the only one that understands Meg completely.

Her brother Levi only knows of the lessons that he gets in observations. What he doesn't understand is that his sister is trying to help him adapt this quality. She knows that he will not be able to have the actual power, per se, but she tries her hardest to teach him observational skills, which could get him closer. But it's all fun and games for Levi.

Her father is just a stubborn man who refuses to believe that such a supernatural trait could even be possible in a human being. Because of this, he has his beliefs that his daughter was not his own. He resents and rejects her. His wife, Bailey, tried to talk to him about it, but to no avail. It would always end in some sort of argument. Meg and her mother eventually gave up trying to convince father and husband of Meg's talents. One day, this would get him in trouble.

Tension was always in the air in the Taylors' house. Bailey loved Bill with all her heart, but it seemed as if she had a second one that went to Meg. Bill's resentment toward Bailey's beloved child caused a tear in the family. Mr. and Mrs. Taylor fought all the time. They always had different
~~~

reasons and subjects to bicker about, but in the end, it always revolved around their firstborn.

Levi, thankfully, was too young to feel the disturbance in the household. Since he never knew of the arguments or their occurrences, due to a loving older sister who cared for his well-being, he never understood.

Meg's attempt of innocence for her baby brother was a loving act, but she feared it would not last long.

She was right.

~~~

"I'm coming…I'm coming! Hold your horses." Lily spoke aloud to her phone as it rang from across the room. She had been in her kitchen cooking dinner and did not hear the cell phone until it was too late. By the time she had finished washing her hands, the ringing had stopped. "Oh well. Don't really care to talk anyway." But she would be forced to, for the phone rang for a second time merely ten seconds later.

"All right! I'll talk. Jeezle Pete's. Hello..?"

"Lily! Finally! What took you so long?"

"Well, I was cooking dinner and had to wash my…"

"Never…never mind. Are…are your parents at home?"

"No, they don't get back for another hour. Wait, are you crying? Meg, are you okay?"

"No. Not at all…this is all my fault…why does this have to be happening to me?"

"Meg, Meg. Breathe…in…out…good. Now tell me what's going on."

"My parents are fighting again, and it's all my fault."

"Oh, honey, no, it's not. They are probably just fighting over the furniture again. It'll settle down soon enough…always does. Wanna crash here for the night?"

"No, it's my fault. Always was, always is… They are throwing the furniture not fighting over it! I tried to hide it from my brother, I did… Now he knows…now he knows, and it's all my fault."
~~~

"Okay, calm down. Please, I beg of you, make logical sense so I can help you."

"Okay…but first you have to promise me something."

"Anything. What is it?"

"You can never repeat what I'm about to tell you."

"Okay…"

"I'm different, Lily. I have this 'gift.' Feels more like a curse though. I have an ability to look at someone and rate how dangerous they are on different levels from one to ten. Levi is a level one, and you are a three. The highest I've ever met was when we went to that police academy, and we saw a few of the criminals being put in the van. One man measured a six. He was a trained soldier who would measure a seven if he was carrying an assault rifle. Now, my own household's rating went from level two to four. Lily, I'm scared. I don't know what to do. Please…help me."

"Whoa, okay. I need to sit down. First off, how does this even make sense?"

"I don't know…I'm just asking you to believe me and not to ask questions now."

"Wait…what level is that kid at school? You know, the one everyone thinks is a potential school shooter, Bennie."

"Ha! Two. He was never a threat. Just likes the attention. He couldn't hurt a fly."

"Oh, thank the heavens! I have to sit next to him in math, and he scares the living beans out of me."

"Can we get back on topic please?"

"Oh, right, right. Okay. So, I totally believe you, Meg. You are my best friend in the entire world. You would never lie to me. But what does your parents' fighting have to do with this?"

"Because my dad resents me for being able to read people. He basically hates me while my mom loves me, so they fight all the time about it. Now they fight over everything to do with me. I've managed to keep their bickering from Levi's attention this entire time, but now he is freaking out all the more because the first time he's ever even thought about Mom and Dad fighting they are throwing lamps at each other! Now he's locked himself in the bathroom, and I can't get him to come out."

"Okay, you guys are going to stay at my house for the next few days. I'm still a little freaked at everything you just told me…but it's actually totally awesome because now you can always protect me, and I will never have to be around anyone dangerous!"

"Lily…"

"Right, I'm focusing. Tell your brother I have ice cream and pizza for him if he comes and spends the night with us. Oh! and we will watch *Hercules*. He loves that movie…that should get him to come out."

"Thanks, you're the best."

"I know."

~~~

"Him?"

"Three." The lunchroom was crowded. This was going to take all day.

"Those two?"

"Both twos. They're idiots, Lily. Do you really expect them to be of any threat to anyone?"

"Well…you never know."

"I'm beginning to wish I never told you." The words rushed out of her mouth but became muffled through her hands, which made a great resting place for her head.

"Well, I'm glad you did!"

Meg had never seen Lily so peppy. If it were possible, she would be bouncing off the walls and doing backflips. All pearly whites showing through her rose red lips. Lily's eyes lit up like stars, and she started slapping Meg's arm—again—in her excitement.

"Ouch!" Meg said, "I already have a bruise there. I would appreciate it if you would stop making it bigger."
~~~

"What about him? No, no! Let me guess… He looks like a one. He is so innocent looking. And come on…he's the new kid!" Lily laughed and patted herself on the back. She soon stopped when she noticed Meg's silence.

"Let's go," Meg pushed.

Lily didn't even think about questioning her. She knew Meg when she got like this.

They were welcomed by a Post-it note attached to Meg's locker.

I've been looking for you
—the New Kid

"Why do you look so pale? How can one note make you look so sick?"

Meg handed her the note while her body slammed against the lockers. Breathless, she murmured the words, "He's a level ten…"

My Journey to Freedom

Sienna Manning

Present day

Tears spring to my eyes as I continue reading old memories in my small tattered journal.

I was so young and innocent, yet I had to live through something no one should experience. I make my way into the kitchen and pour myself a nice, hot cup of coffee. I take a seat at my old wooden table and open my journal.

Most stories start with "once upon a time," but mine is about how just a few weeks ago I was taken from my home in Africa. About how just a few weeks ago I was brought onto a strange ship. And how just a few weeks ago I was told I am a slave. Me, Zemora, a sixteen-year-old slave. So as you can see this isn't the classic "prince in shining armor story," but it might come close.

Memories come flooding back.

Back in time

"I just can't believe it. I am going to spend the rest of my life a slave. Me, Zemora, a sixteen-year-old slave." I finish writing in my journal my father gave me on my fourteenth birthday, just before he left for the sea and never came back. I miss the feel of his strong arms keeping me safe. I miss the sound of his name, Anwar. I like to believe that every page I write he will eventually read. I like to believe he is watching over me and my brothers, Gamba and Garai. I like to believe he is still here.

My father was always one to stay strong. He used to tell me I would always have him by my side and that I shouldn't be afraid. Well, I am afraid. When he took the trip that ended his life, my mother, Imani, became depressed and careless, for she had lost her true love. I remember being the one who reminded her who she really was, that her name means faith, and that she still had us. I never thought I would be taken away.

The howling wind and a splash of cold water on my cheek bring me back to reality. The reality of which I am a prisoner, and I am on a boat that will take me to Alabama where my life will change. Smells of salt water and old wood make me really comprehend that I am not home and I might not be for a long time. I slowly inch across the damp deck toward a pole. The wood beneath my bare feet makes me shiver, and the air stings my patches of skin where my dress is torn. I look toward the bow, the front portion of the boat, and I long to be up there. I long to be up there not as a slave, but as a traveler. I want to be on a voyage where I will get to see the world, but I am not. I am taken from my home onto a boat where I will end up in Alabama. I have a million wishes I want to come true. I want to save my brothers, I want to save myself, and I want to get off this death trap.

Everything around me makes me realize this is my life and it will be for years. I look over and see my brothers, twins. Gamba, tall and strong, almost a complete replica of my father, sits looking at the sea. His short, black hair in the wind. His old clothing now torn to shreds. But most of all I notice the new scars on his neck and more up his arms. The most painful thing I notice is the chain bounding him to the boat. Yet he looks so confident! Like we will all make our way back to Africa. And maybe someday we will. But I know Gamba better than anyone, and beneath the positive look, I see fear.

Garai, my other brother, was always peaceful. He never wanted to fight. He never wanted anything. He believed that we should all be grateful for the life we live. We were very appreciative, but none of us more than Garai. I guess I know how he really feels, for I now realize that there may never be a time where we are all together again. I look over at Garai, and he looks different. His once short hair now longer. His clothes are drained of color, and his skin is more scarred than Gamba's, for he refuses to follow orders. Chained to a pole, he slumps drearily eyed.

I pray Garai will make wise decisions, and one day when we are free, we will all be happy again. I am afraid of losing them. I wouldn't be able to carry on living if they died.

Later in the night, I am starving and parched. I slump to the floor wondering what will become of me. I crawl over to Gamba and Garai. It starts to rain, and the pellets hit our skin, burning our arms. Garai looks up at me and starts to sob. He buries his face in my shirt and cries till there are no more tears. We all sit on the rough boards and just stare at the sky. They drift off to sleep, and a drop of water rolls down my cheek, but I know it is not the rain. I think to myself, not about anything particular. I just think.

I wake up to someone yelling at me and my brothers. "What are you dirty excuses of people doing lying on our deck? Get up and move. Today you will be taken off our watch. Today you officially become a slave."

I can't understand what he is saying. All I hear is yelling. Then all I feel is stinging on my arm. Pain rushes through my body, and my instincts immediately take over, and I throw myself over Gamba and Garai. I shield them from the terrible people who think that whipping, beating, and branding is an okay thing to inflict on us. We are whipped until my skin is raw and bleeding.

After the strange men finish punishing us, we are rushed to a bench where dozens of other Africans sit. We all have looks of fear on our faces. Our legs are bound together, and we cannot move. I look around to make sure no one is watching, then I quickly pull out my journal. My journal was made from a beautiful leather. It had a handmade binding and perfect paper. But now it is tattered and worn out. It is completely different, just like the rest of my life. I push my thoughts aside and write to my father.

Dear Papa,

I don't know what to do. I am trying to shield Gamba and Garai from the terrible life we are now living, I am trying to protect them. I know you always told me not to be afraid, but I can't help it. I am trying to stay strong. Hopefully, you are happy. You and mama always said God watches over us. If he truly is, why is he putting us through this? Gamba and Garai are only fourteen, and we will all be separated. I miss you, I miss mama, and I wish things would just go back to the way they were before. I will stay true to myself. I love you more than the sea. I love you more than the sky. I love you.

Love your daughter,
Zemora

A loud horn signals the boat arrival, and my chest is pounding with anticipation.

"We are approaching the docks!" yells a loud voice overhead.

I whisper a prayer and slowly step into a long line. Slowly one by one, we step off the boat. When I look up, at least a dozen American men and women are staring at us as if we were livestock.

When everyone is off the ship, the auction begins. Someone yanks a young, strong man to his feet and people start bidding.

"Fifty dollars. Anyone for fifty dollars?"

"I will pay fifty dollars," says a man with a top hat.

"One hundred dollars. Do I see a one hundred dollars?"

Another man with black leather shoes steps up. This goes on until the slave in question was sold for eighteen hundred dollars.

I sit with my heart racing when I see both my brothers get pulled up. "What about me? What about me? Let me go with them! Please!" I yell at the top of my lungs while tears all of a sudden stream down my face.

Garai fights back so hard. He is screaming and yelling and using all of his strength when I hear a loud *bang*. I slump to my feet because I know at that moment Garai is gone.

While I am on the floor crying, the wife of a young man stands up and points at me. "I want that one." She pays a thousand dollars up front, grabs her husband, and walks away.

I think I am supposed to follow them, so I yell my sobbing goodbye to Gamba and kiss motionless Garai's cheek. "Goodbye, brother," I whisper.

When I am at the woman's house, I am given a bed and my job. Weeks go by with me doing the same routine. I usually spend my days working with children who will grow up as slaves. At nights, I write in my journal and think about how I lost my brother. I pray for Gamba and weep for Garai.

After about a year, the woman who picked me, Caroline, comes outside where I am hanging clothes and says she needs to meet with me at midnight at the front gate. That night I watch the moon and wonder what Caroline needs to talk to me about. At around 11:55 p.m., I head to the gate. Caroline is waiting for me there with a sack. She explains that she is setting me free, and she has everything I need. Her last words are "You're free. *Run*." I stare at her wide-eyed. Slowly I take the sack and walk past the fence. I never look back.

Present day

I slowly close my journal and look up. A single tear rolls down my face. Here I sit in my own little cottage at age ninety-eight, free. I will never forget my story. I decide to write one last journal entry…

Here I am, Zemora, a ninety-eight-year-old free slave. I have learned that no matter what, you need to believe in yourself. But most of all, never forget your roots because they will help you through your journey.

This is my journey.

—Zemora

Loss

Katherine Lindsey Smith T

It was unnatural.

My trembling hands were pressed against the shaded glass of the viewing section in the operational facility, and my eyes remained glued to the miniscule and deformed figure lying on the table with such a stillness that it seemed as though death had already claimed her.

She had escaped it countless times.

The sharpened blade of the Grim Reaper had hovered above my daughter for so long that I came to know him as an acquaintance, just another spectator to endure the slow death of my daughter, as painful as a heretic burning at the stake and as real as gunshot to the head.

I ached to touch her, to caress her misshapen head, bald from countless surgeries performed by stony medical professionals who had already prepared to grieve.

For many years we had escaped the end, but now the time had come. For her, but also for the part of me that was so hopelessly caught up within her. In an hour, a second, an instant, one strike would kill us both, and we would no longer be fugitives to the underworld.

There were no stages to the process. Instead it was a single prolonged depression destined to end with death.

I used to be afraid.

I used to lie awake at night imagining the absence of life, to cry from eyes nearly swollen shut and let the tears carve their way down my cheeks and collect into one looming puddle of salty water that I wanted to drown in.

Breathing in the almost sweet antiseptic of the white-washed hallway, I watched as the heartbeat of my daughter faded and the brain activity levels plummeted. I watched doctors and nurses turn to me with pity and remorse, and I felt her slip through my fingertips as easily as water.

A psychotic laugh bubbled up from some hidden place inside me; tucked beneath a rib, placed just below the cuticle of my right thumb, and woven into my spine, it burst forth, a giggle, a scream, but mostly a sob.

They say death is part of living, but to me, it was simply the end.

Remember

Huda Haque

When you think about it, when you read the case file, when you look at it logically, it wasn't my fault she was gone. I don't think anyone would ever tell me that it was. Yet, no matter how many times it was said, it felt like the low-lying mass of shame in me would remain for the rest of my life. It made me never want to say her name again. The full impact of the pain still reared its unforgiving head every so often, making me close up to the world even more. It's one of those days.

"Natalie?" Mom knocks on my door tentatively. "Are you all right?"

"No. Please leave me alone." Like always, my palms turn sweaty, and my eyes snap shut as I begin to remember.

Light cascades in throughout my house, like an extravagant ball gown. Outside, a perfect shade of blue dances with clouds, the kind children draw. A familiar array of sounds—the opening of the door, squeaking of sneakers—tells me that Kit is here. Her luminous, glowing smile stretches wider today, as she grabs me in a hug before wildly gesturing to the door.

"We're going outside today, Nat. No question."

Her direct approach still awes me, even though I've known her for years.

"You know I have to ask my mom."

She nods, then falls back on the leather couch with a natural easiness. It's something I've always admired. I, on the other hand, curl into the couch's corner, texting Mom.

"We should do something while waiting for her to reply!" Kit says eagerly, twisting her light brown hair into a ponytail. I laugh.

It isn't going to be more than ten minutes before a reply, and she still wants to fill the time. We sit cross-legged on my bed, drawing and talking. Kit eagerly asks about my day after laughing genuinely at my sarcastic jokes. I bask in the peacefulness that soon gets interrupted by a buzz. "Oh, she said it's fine. Just stay near the house and only for an hour and a half."

Kit rubs her hands together. "Okay, let's go!"

We're soon in a massive forest, my heart thumping wildly with fear. Kit leads the way through twisted paths I've never seen. She keeps glancing back at me, smiling and promising, "You'll love it! I picked this place just for you!"

Time is passing quickly. We've been out fifteen minutes longer than we should have. "Kit," I say firmly, "we have to go. We shouldn't be here. Where are we?"

She whirls around and blinks her emerald eyes, the trees making them shine. She laughs and twirls. "We're in nature, Nat! Take it in and relax. I know my way around."

Looking down at my phone in my hand, I see three missed calls from my parents. *Five more min, we're fine,* I type, sighing at the *WHERE ARE YOU??* that comes buzzing back. Lifting my head, I see green, crownlike treetops and rich brown bark holding it up. Dampness from last night's rain swirls around us as birds chatter away and blazing sunlight pierces through. It *is* beautiful here.

Kit stands next to me, smiling. "I knew you'd love it here, so I brought you. Isn't that what friends are for?"

I say nothing, taking in the scene, but decide otherwise once I see her radiating face again. She did this for me. "Yeah," I breathe. "Only ten more minutes, okay?"

It's been an hour and forty-five minutes over our limit. Twelve missed calls, thirty texts. *Don't worry! We're fine!!!* I type quickly without reading the text when Kit calls to me.

"Nat, It's almost dark, so we can play ultimate hide-and-seek. It's awesome."

I stand up, grinning, and scream, "NOT IT!"

"Fine, fine. You have a minute." Before she starts counting, I eagerly sprint off in the distance, every doubt in my mind gone.

Usually, I would have never agreed to hiding in a forest, but not today. I just feel so free, like Kit. Suddenly, my legs start to ache as I realize I've been standing for a long time. The fear from long ago returns in overpowering waves. "Kit?" I call several times anxiously. Nothing. "KIT!" "KIT! WHERE ARE YOU?" Panic grabs at my throat, and I cannot breathe. A drowning-like sensation overtakes me and becomes worse each time I see a tree without her leaning against it. "KIT!" I scream, the name twisted in anguish. There's nothing left to do here except call for help. Somehow, in my terror, I manage to read through my mom's new frantic texts. *The sheriff is looking for you!!* The glaring screen light is the last thing I see before the memory flashes away.

Next thing I remember, I'm sitting upright in our lonely, stiff wooden chair. The uncomfortable feeling is a welcome distraction from the sheriff's questioning.

"Natalie." He snaps his fingers and sighs as I blink suddenly. Turning to my parents and Kit's, he takes a deep breath. "We think it's a kidnapping. There's actually been several reports of kids disappearing in the state, but we've kept it quiet. We're trying our best, but there's nothing to go off on. That forest is huge, and we've searched every square foot. Again, why did the girls go there? Why—"

I'm deaf to the rest of his remarks, the cries of sorrow for Kit, and the shouts of anger that the kidnappings were hushed up. It's like I'm underwater. Nothing registers with me quite like the word "nothing."

Nothing—that's what's left of my best friend. My sister. Why? She was gone because of the very thing that made her Kit. Her free spirit, constantly adventurous soul. Gone, just like that. I want to hate her for making me hate myself, but I can't. I could never. So instead, I made her a stranger in my own mind.

Sweat drips on me, and my eyes open. It's over. Heavy, deep breaths come in surges.

"Sweetie? It's time to go to bed. Remember, first day of school tomorrow! Goodnight, sleep tight!"

My parents knock cautiously on my door, and I quickly reply. "Okay, goodnight. Love you." I could sleep for centuries, my body is so drained. It's always like this, but today there's an added layer of anxiety. School. My first year without her. Nervous thoughts flutter in my head and get stopped only by the overwhelming allure of sleep.

~~~

"Welcome! I'm so excited to start a great year," the hawkish teacher says with a plastered grin.

"Well, that makes one of us," a brown-haired girl chuckles softly to me.

Surprised, I turn to her. I wasn't even planning on talking today. "Hi. I'm Mattie," she says, smiling. Her eyes burn a fierce shade of green, nearly blinding.

"W-we shouldn't be talking," I stutter, turning away. From the corner of my vision, I see hurt on her face, but ignore it.

At lunch, my table is pleasantly lonely. My faraway thoughts cause me to stare unblinkingly at the maroon wall. "Reminds you of fall, doesn't it?" Kit used to say, but now it looks like rotten tomatoes smashed together. I feel my fist leaving a red imprint on my leaning cheek and couldn't care less. Actually, I couldn't care at all about any of this. The void could swallow me whole right now, and I'd thank it. As I laugh bitterly to myself thinking about it, someone slides in front of me. The annoying girl from first period, grinning.

Too lazy to move away, I ask sharply, "What're you doing here?"

"You seemed like you needed a friend," she replies, getting comfortable at the table. I stare as she spreads her lunch out and smirk.
~~~

"Huh. If only you knew."

"Well, I don't. So I'm trying to. Maybe I should start with asking you your name, *huh*?" Her voice is unflinching, but warm.

"Natalie," I say shortly.

"Pretty. Can I call you Nat?"

Every time Kit called me that comes rushing back, and I close my eyes, overwhelmed. Tears push against my eyelids ferociously.

"Are...you okay?"

I look straight at Mattie. "Don't ever call me that."

She recoils, then resumes sticking her face in mine. "I don't know what happened to you...but you need to face it. Maybe you need to talk."

Sickening silence settles over me, and lunch ends. I don't talk for the rest of the school day.

~~~

My wall greets my head as I slide down and sit quietly on my room floor. I feel naked, exposed. A complete stranger just saw through me. Her firm words had cut through my inner barrier, and I know it. *Face it,* she had said. How? I refused to say Kit's name out loud, refused to think about anything related to her other than that night. She has become the symbol of the worst time in my life. That's all she is now.

Shame grips me, so hard I almost become dizzy. Not the familiar kind that had made me responsible for that night, but the shame for forgetting *her.* Her smile, her laugh, her jokes. Her easy manner, her way of making you feel like the most important person in the world. The hundreds of memories had been shoved away to spare my selfish self. I close my eyes like always, but this time I don't remember that night, I remember the years I had spent with her.

It feels like forever before I open my tear-filled eyes. I'm laughing, my heart filled to the brim. The abrupt swing of the door barely startles me.

"Are you okay, Natalie?" my parents ask, concerned.
~~~

Another laugh escapes me, and I nod happily.

"Yeah," I say, wiping my eyes. "I just miss her so much. I miss…Kit."

The Laptop

Arriyannah Herring

"Beige? Is that you? Beige! Don't come any closer, please!"

I heard my older sister beg me, which brought me to tears, but despite my own wounded shoulder I did not waver. I kept limping toward the tub as fast as I could. When red liquid swam around my trembling feet, I already knew.

Still, I did not stop walking.

"Beige, please. Just leave. You can't help me now. I don't want you to see me like this." Saige's voice was no longer strong and demanding. It was no longer the voice I grew up with. Now, it was barely a whisper. A faint croak.

I kept hobbling as fast as I could.

A second later I stood in front of her tub, looking at the blood covering my sister's injured body like a blanket. I didn't see where the gunshot was. Possibilities of how she ended up this way in the tub played in my mind, and terror ripped through my veins like poison. I was a stone for only a second but then ran to my bed and grabbed my phone and dialed 911 with trembling hands. I let out my words with a rush, like a boulder was in the back of my throat rolling down my tongue, pushing the words along with it. They asked me questions that I couldn't understand, and I told them answers that probably didn't apply to their questions. They immediately started, but the surprise snowstorm outside wasn't in our favor. I frantically called my dad, and all I could scream was, "Come home, Saige is dying."

I then ran to the bathroom and slid across the floor through the blood, half crawling, half walking, and lifted up my sister's head. My injured shoulder cried out in pain, but my body felt numb. Only my heart was in real pain.

"We have to get you out of here," I said, frantically trying to lift her up by her arms. I could feel Saige's body working against my wish. Saige had already accepted the fact that she might die. But she couldn't die. A world without her was not a world I wanted to live in. We would go to therapy together and support each other as we got over this traumatic incident. This would bring us even closer than before. Saige would not end here…

~~~

"Beige, we need to get you your own laptop one day, so that you won't use mine," Saige said to me. I smiled. I had been using her laptop for over a year to do schoolwork and write mini stories. She always understood that I needed to use writing as a way to escape the real world. It felt so amazing being able to feel all of the emotions of a made-up character and make-believe their lives. It was like I was the creator of all life and the most powerful being in the world. It helped when I felt powerless in the world I lived in.

"You don't have to do that for me. Once I get a job, I promise I'll get my own," I reassured her.

"Oh, you definitely will. I'm not paying for it. *You* are. When I said 'we,' I meant that you buy it, but I help pick it out."

"Fine. Whatever." I rolled my eyes and started to write my last sentence. Saige laughed.

"I'm kidding. I promise that I'll get you a laptop. As a way to remind you that I'll be there whenever you cry. Even when I am not around."

"That doesn't make sense, Saige, and how can I be reminded of that from a laptop?"

She laughed again. "I don't know, Beige. I just feel like that would be something that you would want to hear."

"Whatever."

You could say my sister was my favorite family member.

But she was more.
~~~

Every time a friend would hurt me or do something unpredictable that would leave me in pain, my sister was the one to comfort me. My mom was always busy. My dad didn't understand and would always say things like, *Just forget about them.* My brothers were…brothers.

Saige was the colorful building blocks, and I was the dull stone surrounding her that kept her from falling. I had the brains. She always made irrational decisions that I had to talk her out of, like robbing a gas station with her very bad, influential friends. Or going to the movies with a guy named Chainsaw. Also, walking up to a complete stranger's car because he said he had food in the back seat he was selling to families around the neighborhood to support breast cancer, but he hadn't looked like the type to support such a cause.

While I was the stone that surrounded her and kept her from tumbling over, she was the colorful building blocks from within me that gave my dull life meaning. I prevented the bad, and she encouraged the good.

But there was one mistake that I couldn't prevent.

Alan Jugo.

~~~

I remember seeing him for the first time at an amusement park. My family had been planning to go for what felt like forever, and Saige wanted to introduce her boyfriend to the family.

He was handsome. Tall, big eyes with long eyelashes, and a very amazing skill—he could act. That was what he did the whole time he was there—pretend. He acted as if he loved my sister. He acted as if he wanted no other girl but my sister. He didn't even look at pretty girls walking by. He really fooled my parents.

I walked alongside my two brothers, Christopher and Evan. Chris was a cool eldest brother. He let us do whatever we wanted but still managed to make all of his younger siblings treat him as a third parent. Evan was the complete opposite—more reckless than Saige, not respected by or
~~~

respective of anyone. He was the youngest. Still, they both were as much a home to me as Saige.

Alan Jugo didn't try to win me over like he had done with my brothers. He'd asked Chris if the three boys could go on this scary ride that Saige was too afraid to get on. As soon as the ride was over, they all came out laughing, and Chris did that guy thing where they nod heads or something like that to show Alan was accepted by my hard-to-impress brother.

I was still suspicious. Saige's relationships had not ended well in the past. Half of them our parents didn't even know about. Saige definitely didn't know how to pick them. Alan Jugo couldn't have been any different.

But then in the evening, when we were walking back to the parking lot, my stupidity got the best of me. I ended up running out into the street on instinct when the basketball my little brother won for me dropped out of my hands and rolled into the busy parking lot. I bent down to pick it up, but instead, was confronted by a humongous Jeep that couldn't stop fast enough. Everything happened in a weirdly focused blur—the Jeep appearing suddenly in my view, trying to stop, Alan getting there fast to wrap his arms around my waist to throw both of us onto the sidewalk.

The basketball was crushed by the Jeep's shiny black tires. The Jeep stopped, and a head stuck out to ask if we were okay and say that he was sorry. The middle-aged man with squinted eyes and curly brown hair inside of the Jeep seemed very nice. I could've just ruined his whole day, but I couldn't do much to help him since my whole family was petting me like a dog and thanking Alan and telling me I was stupid for going into the street to retrieve the basketball, and that I ought to be thankful to Alan for saving my life. I won't lie. At the time, I'd fallen for my sister's boyfriend and was completely okay with accepting him into the family.

Months went by. My sister and her boyfriend were happy, and my parents were convinced that he was a good influence on her since they hadn't gotten any calls from the police station because of her since Alan came into her life. My brothers hung out with him, and Alan sometimes gathered around the dinner table to eat and talk with us like we'd known each other our entire lives. However, Alan never talked about his own life much, only small stories about the good times that he'd had with his family and facts about his parents, like their occupations.

Everyone adored Alan, including me.

Until I didn't.

Until I saw a different side of Alan that I was not supposed to see.

A side he most likely would've never shown to my other family members or me if he had the choice.

My parents had wanted to go to the movie theater to see this horror film. Chris and Evan decided to go with them because if they didn't they had to clean the whole house. I was going to go to my friend Leona's house so that I didn't have to go with them. Saige wanted to stay home. She told me why—so that she could be alone with Alan. I, being an obedient sister at the time, promised not to tell our parents about this arrangement, so I allowed my sister to stay in our house alone, claiming that she had a project in English class that she had to finish. My parents understood and decided to allow her to stay home alone because they were convinced that she wouldn't cause destruction based on her recent record.

I threw on some comfortable clothes to walk half a block to Leona's house after my parents and my two brothers had left for the movie theater. As I was about to leave, I heard a faint knock on the door downstairs. I knew it was Alan and not my parents because of the way he'd knock on the door. Three fast knocks, then a pause, then two more knocks. I assumed Saige didn't know I was still there, since I had forgotten to tell her that I wasn't going to the movie. I decided to make a quick exit to the door once they were both out of sight.

"You came here fast. Come in," I heard Saige's voice say, then a door close. I peered down the white-carpeted stairs and made my first few steps when I saw that the area around the door directly in front of the staircase was vacant. Just when I was halfway down the steps, I heard glass break. I stopped, frozen, wondering if they had heard me and grabbed onto the railing, looking over it to find myself staring at the back of Alan and the scared look on Saige. I wanted to see what was going on but didn't want to overreact. The broken glass on the ground scattered around both Alan's and Saige's feet. I could see a bit of blood on Saige's foot. Could it have been an accident? The look on Saige's face could've been because they had broken Mom's favorite glass vase.

My innocent claim was proved invalid when Alan grabbed Saige by the shoulders and pushed her up against the wall with force enough to throw a cow across a field. He let go, and Saige fell to the ground. Alan turned to the broken glass and looked down at it with rage in his eyes. I clenched my hands into fists and bit my lip so hard I felt a metallic taste on my tongue. I started to walk down the stairs when I found Saige looking directly at me. She shook her head a bit as if to say, *Don't.* I ignored her warning and stepped cautiously down another step. This time, she mouthed, "No," and shook her head even more. I stepped down yet another step.

"No." She said it out loud this time.

"Shut up!" Alan said.

I stopped. Alan was still unaware of my presence when he turned to Saige. I knew we both couldn't fight him. But I had to find a way to save Saige, so I fished my phone out of my pocket. I wanted to call the police, but there were many things that could've gone wrong with that, so I instead pressed the camera button and hit record. Saige's eyes widened at me for half a second when she forced them away and looked up at Alan. I slowly stepped up another step, then another, making sure I wouldn't be seen by him. Alan started to yell at Saige and scream sentences and words that I couldn't identify. He cursed between every syllable that came out of his mouth. I was holding up the recorder the whole time, trembling viciously. Saige tried to stand up, but Alan slapped her in the face, and she fell back down. The phone trembled in my hands. A small sound escaped my throat, and I prayed that he didn't hear. With all the commotion he was causing, he didn't.

He continued to speak. His words became more clear, and I realized Saige hadn't done anything wrong. He was mad because she'd hesitated when he had asked if she loved him. At that moment, I knew he was crazy. I felt nauseous. How could our whole family have been so clueless? We allowed a psycho into our house and smiled in his face with such sincerity.

Saige got up and lifted her arms to him cautiously. "I love you, okay? Is that what you wanted to hear? Fine then."

Alan must've hated her comment, because he slapped her again, causing her to stumble backward. He walked toward her, with too much energy. I knew he was going to cause her more harm, and the rage that had been bubbling up inside of me couldn't take anymore. I pressed the stop button on my phone and slid the evidence into my pocket.

"Hey!" I yelled, my voice surprisingly powerful. Alan turned around, and I watched with rage as his dark, lifeless eyes widened with surprise. He regained composure, and with a dark voice, he threatened me.

"You go right back upstairs and erase everything from your mind. If you don't, I will hurt both you and your sister."

"Sure, go ahead. I'd love to show the judge more evidence. Even though the video that I just recorded is evidence enough," I said as I watched my sister pick up a knife and walk closer to her boyfriend.

"What did you just say?" Alan said, stepping closer to me.

I stepped down another step, afraid and surprisingly courageous at the same time. Before I could speak, Saige screamed and did something that I could not see clearly. I knew what she did though. I knew exactly what she did when Alan fell forward and grabbed the back of his neck. Saige ran to me and took my hand, and together, we raced out of the house and down the street.

Alan was arrested with a small injury on his neck.

Everything went back to normal—or close to normal—after a few months.

But it didn't stay normal for more than two years, because one day, Saige busted into my room crying.

"He called me, Beige! He called me! His father got him out."

Instantly, my stomach churned. I wanted badly to think that she was talking about someone else, but we did not know anyone besides Alan who had ever been in jail.

"What did he say?" My voice was trembling, and I didn't try to hide it. This was more serious than before. If I were Alan, crazy mind and all, I wouldn't let the people who put me in jail get away.

"He said that he is coming for me…and you. I have to find a way to protect you and get you out of this mess. But…" Tears started to fall down Saige's face.

"We have to alert the authorities and tell Mom and Dad," I suggested, fighting the fear creeping inside of me. I had to be the stronger one. We would die if both of us were afraid.

"What can Mom and Dad do? What can the authorities do? They aren't going to put him back in jail until he *actually* does something wrong. And they might send us to a witness protection program or something. I'm not allowing my whole family to live undercover because of a twenty-two-year-old man." She burst out crying, and I hugged her.

Mom and Dad were downstairs, and Chris and Evan were in their rooms. I hoped that they didn't hear Saige's outburst. Saige was right. If Mom and Dad heard about what happened, they would only pick a rational solution. But it was Alan we were dealing with. It would take more than a rational solution to fix an irrational problem.

"Saige, keep quiet. They might hear," I pleaded.

Saige sat down of the floor of the room we shared and wiped her eyes, sniffling. I blinked a few times to push the tears threatening to flow into my brown eyes.

"We will get through this, Saige. Don't worry," I said.

"We have to go. We can't stay here," Saige said, sniffling.

"We will find a way."

Saige and I sat there for a few silent moments. It was the last time we had peace together.

A few days went by. Then it was Sunday, Easter morning, and my family was at church while Saige and I decided to stay home. Saige and I were still very shaken from the call we'd received from Alan. I'd gotten back into the habit of writing stories. I had been working on the climax of one of them. It was a story about a majestic princess who saved her kingdom from falling into a darkness caused by a witch, her mother. I loved making fictional stories the most because my imagination didn't have to be limited by reality.

Saige passed by me and rolled her eyes when she saw that I was on her laptop. I goofily smiled at her.

"What are you working on?"

"Oh, I'm working on this—"

There was a knock on the door. Saige and I froze.

"You think the church service let out early today?"

"No, as a matter of fact, the service should be longer since they have Easter egg hunting afterward."

"Should I answer the door?" Saige questioned.

"I don't know," I replied truthfully.

"I'll go alone," she said.

"No, let's go together."

We walk down the stairs and to the door.

"Who is it?" I yelled, my heart trembling.

"It's me, Leona."

I heard Leona's voice, and my heart finally relaxed. I must've forgotten Leona mentioning that she'd come over. I still didn't remember, but there were a lot of things I had forgotten the week of the call.

I opened the door and was greeted by a terrified Leona with sweat beads rushing down the sides of her face. At first, I only saw her, until, one by one, different images came into focus: arms wrapped around her neck, a jet-black gun pointed at her head, and a man standing beside her, holding the gun.

Alan.

Saige looked like she was about to close the door when Alan barged in, still holding Leona, and closed the wood door behind him.

Saige grabbed my hand and pulled me behind her.

"Oh, don't worry about your little sister. I only want you for now." Alan smirked and pushed Leona toward us.

Leona, who still had her pajamas on and messy burgundy-dyed hair, ran behind Saige and took my arm.

"Are you okay?" I cried, feeling guilty, as if it was my fault she was involved in this.

"I'm…fine," she said. Though from the look on her face, I knew she was not.

"Leave them alone, Alan." Saige's voice was more powerful than I expected, despite the gun Alan was holding safely by his side.

"I will, if you tell me something," Alan said.

"What?"

Alan held the gun up to Saige's head. "Tell me you love me."

"NO!" I cried and jumped in front of Saige.

She tried to pull me back behind her, but it was too late. Alan pulled the trigger, and I felt like my shoulder had just been torn off my body. Pain surged through my whole body like shocks, not just because of the gunshot, but because of the hard floor that I hit when I fall down. Saige and Leona rushed to both sides of me. The world started to turn black, but before I could get my rest, I saw Alan dragging the screaming, kicking Saige away from me. Up the stairs and out of sight.

Usually in a movie, you'd wake up in a hospital bed. First you'd see black, then you'd see white, and then you'd see doctors in long white coats holding clipboards and writing things down and family members getting up once they see you opening your eyes. You'd see people crying and a few others asking the doctor about your condition. You'd see a bunch of different tools around you and then you would sit up and look at your hands once your eyesight becomes clear, and you'd fall back with joy once you realize that you've just cheated death and that you are not in the afterlife, but in the hospital bed.

I did not wake up in a hospital, nor did I feel I cheated death.

Instead, I was right where I was before, on the ground. Leona knelt beside me. It seemed she was regaining her consciousness as well.

"Beige?" Her voice was a mere whisper, but when I regained full consciousness and I met her eyes, Leona nervously hugged me.

"Where is Saige?" I asked.

"I don't know. I think she is upstairs."

I hastily stood up and felt the burn within my shoulder.

Leona's voice became softer. "Beige, I don't know what happened up there. You may want to get help before going upstairs."

"She is *my* sister. Don't tell me what to do when it comes to her." I rushed upstairs while Leona ran outside to get some help.

That was when I saw Saige in her bathroom tub—broken and unable to move a muscle. I could've saved her. I realized that I might lose her. I realized that I already did.

~~~

Alan was sentenced to life in prison without bail. He admitted to kidnapping Leona, shooting me in the shoulder,
~~~

and murdering Saige. He even explained the way he did it in detail. He made Saige sound like a hero, which she was, but those words coming from him always echoed in my mind and made me want to walk right up into that prison with a knife.

I told my mother about it, and she only cried and hugged me and wouldn't let go. I didn't cry though. My family never saw a tear go down my face after Saige's death. I don't know why. It felt like all the tears left my body on the day of her death.

I didn't go to the funeral.

I stayed home, in our room, and looked through all of Saige's things. I knew my family understood that I couldn't be in that terrible setting, not after what I saw, so they allowed me to stay home and have my own little funeral. When they left, I let loose, and I cried loudly and freely, threw things, and went into the bathroom where she'd died, and I threw things in there as well. My parents wanted to board the bathroom up. They even suggested moving out, but my brothers and I didn't want to let this change our lives for the worse. We'd only be running away from something that would follow us everywhere we went. You can't escape loss.

Warm, salty tears stung my eyes, made my cheeks itchy, and made me hiccup and sniffle. I felt like I was going to die being there in that bathroom, so I locked the bathroom door and told myself that I would never enter it again. And so I resumed playing the role of a patient in a psychiatric hospital. I went to the desk where the laptop lay and looked underneath it to see what else I could throw. Nothing was underneath the desk except for a large box wrapped in shiny purple wrapping paper. It stood out so much that I was surprised I hadn't realized it was there. I pulled it out and examined it. There was nothing on it that said who it was for or what it could be, so I carefully peeled the wrapping paper off, my tears no longer streaming down my face, but staining it. Under the wrapping paper was a cardboard box with a note on it.

Beige,

After I got the call from Alan, I stayed up all night and read some of your stories while you slept. I loved them so much and hated that I never showed enough interest in your talents. I never told this, but I was always jealous of you. I was the screw-up that still couldn't grasp right from wrong, even at eighteen years of age. But you knew what you wanted and knew what life meant and knew right from wrong since you were a kid. I'm a terrible older sister. I put you in harm's way, and now my screw-ups are coming back to haunt both me and you. I came to the conclusion that I would show you how much I cared and love you. I'll do everything that I can to show that I love you, so don't ever give up on your dreams. I finally realized now that all I want in the world is for my sister to be smarter than me and live a happier life. Beige, I love you, and I always will. And because I love you so much, I used everything I had to get this for you. The best thing I could get to show how I feel and tell you what I want to tell you, not through the letter, but through the heart. So I got you this. Open it.

Saige

I held the letter to my heart, tears streaming. I opened up the box.

A laptop. An expensive, new laptop that must've cost a fortune.

At first I didn't know what she meant by telling me through the heart, not through the letter. But then I could hear her words loud and clear as our conversation from months ago reemerged from my brain and traveled to my soul:

"I promise that I'll get you a laptop. As a way to remind you that I'll be there whenever you cry. Even when I am not around."

Restless Fingers

Rachel Zhang

The fan installed in my laptop was relentlessly working to return its temperature to normal. Considering how long I'd been typing away on my keyboard, I knew it would take days until my laptop wasn't scalding to the touch. For a split second, I glanced up from my screen only to find myself encircled by a hundred screaming boys. The smell that ensued after sitting in a humid room with all males, who evidently weren't taught the importance of bathing, was similar to the inside of a deceased organism—but my attention soon returned to the task at hand. Finishing the last line of code, I hit the "Enter" button in satisfaction.

With arrogant simplicity, I stated, "Done."

My statement left a hundred mouths hanging open and provoked a few minor strokes. The faces of my fellow competing hackers were vibrant red and dripping in sweat as they gaped at me.

"That's impossible. How did you hack into the system that quickly?" one boy questioned.

In a brisk movement, I swung my bag over my shoulder and headed toward the door.

"See ya tomorrow, losers!" I shouted behind me.

~~~

I caught my customary five o'clock bus ride home and picked the front row window seat. Leaning my cheek against the ice-cold glass as we drove through the city was the highlight of my day. I marveled at the city's skyline, and the
~~~

warmth of the bus was enough to make me question life's privileges. The motor emitted a toxic smell, yet it was still more desirable than that of a room filled with teenage boys. I chuckled under my breath thinking of the predicament I left them with: a girl surpassed them in "their" game. Despite their malnourished social awareness, I genuinely enjoyed their company and found inexplicable joy in disproving their assumptions, which prompted me to start hacking. Computer hacking was like a chemical bond holding us all together; it obscurely coursed through our veins, making our fingers itch to touch the keyboard. Technology was viewed as a "man's" craft, but those boys permitted my presence; they recognized my talent and didn't care to deny it. My thoughts were interjected by a woman's voice.

"Excuse you!" she said accusingly to the bus driver.

The old driver's elbow moved swiftly away from the young woman's bottom as she was getting off at the last stop. Had my eyes not been so attentively trained to search for miniscule coding errors, I wouldn't have noticed his subtle movement.

"Sorry, ma'am, I was just reaching for the glove box."

He followed his apology with a smirk, as if it was mockery. The woman scoffed and demanded he apologize "without the sarcasm." By now everyone else had disembarked at this last stop.

The driver peered cautiously behind his leather chair at the empty bus and hauled the woman toward him.

"Listen, sweetheart, I've been at this job for decades now. This whole town knows and likes me. You tell anyone about this little incident, and they'll fire you from your precious job for false accusations. Got it?" he stated with unprecedented fire behind his eyes.

His stance exuded dominance over her; he leaned tauntingly forward and kept one hand clenched onto her waist. The woman's fearsome stare suddenly melted away, and her eyes brimmed with tears. She quickly nodded and sprinted out the bus door, her pink dress flowing behind her. Here was a woman, who I'd always perceived to be nothing but dauntless, surrendering to the single threat of Bill the bus driver. I was completely dumbfounded. My feet reluctantly began to move toward the exit, pulling the remains of my body along with it. He hadn't noticed my presence until now and was a bit taken aback to see a witness of his behavior.

"Bye, sweetie!" he called after me as I was rushing out. All these years, I regarded that phrase as a sign of mere friendliness, but now I had a different impression.

For the first time, I whipped my head around, looked audaciously into Bill's eyes, and said, "Don't call me that," and left in a hurry.

~~~

My nimble fingers fumbled through my bag, as I tried to find my seemingly impalpable keys. Finally, I crawled through the small dorm room window and relieved my back from the barbaric load it had endured all day. The janitor's room was dull and carried layers of smell—expectantly so, considering the college's low budget. Nevertheless, all I required was a small cot and heater to help me survive the bitter east coast winter. Having been a foster child, I was already fortunate enough that Douglas, our local community college's head janitor, adopted me as legal guardian and let me stay with him after I was put on "temporary expulsion" for hacking into the college's student profiles. I referred to my actions as "child's play" when the entire college board confronted me. Their
~~~

firewalls were just like Douglas's vintage '90s overalls: comical and cheap.

The door opened, and Douglas trudged in. "Oh, there you are. I was about to look for you," he said as he rubbed his tense neck. Douglas worked a nine-hour shift six days a week as a janitor. He cleaned up after the filthiest of kids, and even after thirty years, all he had to show for it were callused hands and a slim bank account. Although this rubbed my temperamental nature the wrong way, Douglas always kept his composure.

"Douglas?" I asked, pretending to be occupied searching through my army-green canvas bag.

He removed his ancient, and hardly sanitary, baseball cap.

"Uh-huh?"

"Are you familiar with—uh—Bill the bus driver?" I questioned casually.

"That old drunkard? Oh yeah I know 'im. Why?"

"Nothing. I just noticed something weird today."

With that ambiguous statement, Douglas was wide awake, and I continued to tell my story. After I finished, with my occasional digressions from the topic, he rubbed his temple.

"Was my narrative so poignant that it's moved you to a loss of words?" I quipped.

"No. I'm not worried about Bill or his victim."

"How could you possibly say that?"

"Listen, kid. Stuff like that has been happening for a long time now. I'm just anxious knowing that you'll take this matter into your own hands."

I smirked and reached for my laptop, which glistened in the mischievous moonlight that crept through our small window.

~~~

As I woke, the sound of college students bolting to their classes resonated within the walls. I needed a minimal amount of time to regroup myself and bolt out the window. The crisp air embraced my body and brought a lingering silence with it. For a split second, I was not one of seven billion people on Earth; I was something more noticeable—the moon kindling the waves instead of a stone commencing a ripple. My bliss was interrupted by a police officer.

"I'm sorry, Miss, but you'll have to follow us."

I fought my instinct of running and submitted to the orders.

They took me to the town's courthouse where my "fate" was to be examined and voted upon.

~~~

As I entered the courtroom, I saw that Douglas was seated near the front row, and Bill the bus driver was conversing with the judge. My bewilderment continued when I turned to see that all the seats were filled. The "maximum capacity" sign near the front door seemed to be a mere suggestion instead of the law.

"All right, we now begin the case! All be seated!" the judge hollered, smashing her gavel hard.

No one cared to give me an explanation, so I whispered to Douglas from a reasonable distance. All I managed to understand was: "Bill," "in trouble," and "you." I realized that this trial was my word against the local bus driver's.

"Miss Erin Stewart has released private information from Mr. Bill Bushwin's laptop revealing sexual messages he exchanged with a minor. She then went on to state on her blog that Mr. Bushwin touched Miss Georgia Tuft inappropriately on the five o'clock bus ride yesterday. Care to respond, Mr. Bushwin?" the judge said.

"Your honor, I've worked for this community for decades. I've known you since I first started working here. Do you truly think that these allegations are true? For God's sake, the only witness you have is a twenty-year-old girl! She's delusional! She was probably wasted."

"Is that all you have to say?" the judge asked.

Bill nodded and drew back to his table.

"Your honor, I don't drink, nor am I delusional. I have two healthy eyes. Nevertheless, this was my first experience with sexual harassment. I'm not an expert, but I'm aware that the law guarantees safety and security, regardless of who you are. I'm not sure shoving your hand up someone's skirt exhibits safety, but who knows? Maybe I'm 'too young' to define respect so boldly," I fired back.

"Thank you," the judge responded.

I sunk into my large armchair in exasperation, and I questioned why we were here. Did we not have full access to the bus security cameras? If the technology was too complicated for the security department, I would happily provide them with assistance. But I knew that wasn't why we were here. So why were we? Why waste a perfectly fine afternoon deliberating a matter that could easily be resolved with a video tape? Then it struck me: we weren't here for a trial at all. It was not for legal purposes, but to shine a spotlight on this issue—to make a statement. I searched the room for the only person that the judge undoubtedly needed to hear from.

To my joy, as I came out of my thoughts, I saw Georgia Tuft walking to the trial room. Her testimony agreed with mine. The bus driver was sentenced to eleven months in prison.

About Lune Spark Books

Lune Spark Books aims to encourage children to engage in creating writing. We work with parents and young writers to promote creative fiction writing to help identify talent. We run annual competitions and creative writing classes and publish short stories by the young writers. For more details, visit us at http://lunespark.com/youngwriters/.

For the details of the contest or to enroll in the contest, please visit us at
http://lunespark.com/youngwriters/storycontest/.

Follow us on social media to keep up with the latest updates:
https://www.facebook.com/youngwriterscontest/
https://twitter.com/LuneSparkLLC

Other Books by Lune Spark

On Writing Wonderfully (Writing reference)

(Age: 10+ years)

The script of Pawan Mishra's talk to Lady Shri Ram College, which has since become a popular reference for students of creative writing and aspiring writers.

A Window to Young Minds (Short stories)

(Age: 10+ years)

This book is the first of the Lune Spark Short Story Contest's yearly anthologies and includes twenty-five award-winning short stories by young writers.

Surviving Gretchen (Fiction, family, friendship)

(Age: 8–12 years)

Thick as thieves since birth, Abby and Emma aren't just best friends. They're like two life-forces sharing the same soul. Then a pretentious prima donna of a girl named Gretchen blows into their lives. Will Abby and Emma survive Gretchen?

Coinman (Fiction, humor, satire, office parody)

(Age: 13+ years)

Coinman is one of life's victims, the receiver of subtle bullying in an office environment and thinly disguised control in his own home, but he remains true to his desire to be polite and accepting of how he is treated by everyone. Then an incident at work changes all that.

Speaking Up for Each Other (Short stories for tweens and middle grade readers)

(Age: 10–13 years)

Wonderfully wide-ranging, original, and enjoyable, this outstanding collection features twenty-four short stories like That Glowing Penny, in which a helpless girl has to live in fear of her own family.

My Teacher Hilda (Picture book series)

(Age: 3–8 years)

Playing is an important part of children's learning and development. Appropriate for children in the age range of three to eight years, this book series focuses on play-based early learning. The cute animal characters continuously engage in fun-filled activities that help children learn.

Nora's First Day at School

The Water Balloon Fight

A Picnic Day

The Lemonade Stand

Mother's Day

www.ingramcontent.com/pod-product-compliance
Lightning Source LLC
Chambersburg PA
CBHW051705180726
48283CB00004B/1215
* 9 7 8 1 9 4 7 9 6 0 2 0 6 *